TIME AFTER TIME

THREE LIVES CONNECTED BY ONE
INCREDIBLE DISCOVERY

TIME

AFTER

TIME

VICTOR WATSON

The Book Guild Ltd

First published in Great Britain in 2022 by
The Book Guild Ltd
Unit E2 Airfield Business Park,
Harrison Road, Market Harborough,
Leicestershire. LE16 7UL
Tel: 0116 2792299
www.bookguild.co.uk
Email: info@bookguild.co.uk
Twitter: @bookguild

Typeset in 11pt Minion Pro

Printed and bound in Great Britain by CMP UK

ISBN 978 1915352 385

British Library Cataloguing in Publication Data.
A catalogue record for this book is available from the British Library.

To my wife Judy, loyal, diligent, and challenging.

1

THE FIRST TIME

I was a girl-boy. I was a boy-girl.

I was alone. And a long way from home.

There was a wood, still and frozen in winter twilight. I found a fox-path through the trees, narrow and dark. It was hard for feet to follow. It was black in the wood. The trees were inside my head, and my thoughts were branches.

I saw deer standing in the shadows like spirits of the dead.

A brown bird watched me as I passed through the trees. Its eye was bright, its legs were twigs. It was two hand's-breadths from my eyes, like a secret. It was in my head. It knew I was a girl-boy.

There was no-one but me in the dark quiet world. And the small bird, watching with her bright eye. And the deer, gentle in the shadows, not moving, alert to danger.

'Will there be danger?' I'd asked.

'There is always danger,' he said.

The path faded and the trees thinned. I came out of the wood under the open frosty sky. There was a stream, shining, cold, talking softly. And a grassy place, resting and still.

The stream and the grass and the frost were inside my thoughts.

They belonged to me. The first stars shone in the purple sky. And they were mine too.

My name is Sæwara.

I had left the old man cooking at the fire, the story-teller. He always cooked at night-fall. I was his companion.

I had left him beside the fire, under the bright stars, wrapped in skins. Guthlac the minstrel, the story-maker, spinner of tales. He pinned his cloak around his body with a golden brooch. At the edge of a wood I left him, cooking.

No-one saw me. No-one knew me. I was a boy-girl and I was a girl-boy.

Something had drawn me away. Guthlac sighed and said, 'Go! The young are foolish, the old are weary.'

That was the way he spoke. He was an old man. I honoured him in my heart but I had left him, cooking. And alone.

*

I stepped out of the trees. Across the stream, humped in the grass, I saw a place of fear. Not the battle-fear of heroes, but the night-fear of travellers.

I was a girl, and I was a boy. And I was a story-seeker. So I waded the stream.

It was a sharp toe-biter. I stepped out of the water and walked across the frozen grass towards the place of fear. Its walls were hard stone, and roofless. There were doorways where the cold wind went in.

We knew these places. We kept clear of their power. People said they were built by Roman giants. We had heard of the Romans. Their power had failed. Their halls had been built by gods who were mad. Only a god would have the strength. Only a mad god would make a high cliff for the side of a house.

It was a place of dread from the dark generations, an unknown time that was not ours. Guthlac said there were whole towns of them, empty of people, empty of stories. They stood, silent, haunted by dead Romans who once lived there.

Why did they build stone caves to live in? Towering above the land! Were they stone-mad?

They were not of our race, the mad giant Romans. Their past was not joined to our time. Guthlac said they came, they made strange and terrible buildings, then they went away.

They left – and we crossed the grey winter-dark sea.

I stepped close to the place of fear and held out my hand. I touched the mountain-house with my fingers, the stone-madness of the Roman gods. I stood under the darkening star-way and listened to the mad god-house breathing its old Roman nightmares.

Then fear seized me and I ran back into the woods. I

turned my back on the place of dread and went back to Guthlac. The trees of the wood were blacker than the sky. The earth under my feet was stone-hard.

*

Guthlac grunted. An old man's greeting. We ate.

In the frost-quiet we heard men's voices, from afar in the cold night. Then, after a long stillness, the voices spoke again, closer.

After sunset, after moonset, danger. Firelight draws travellers, unknown men and women, seeking warmth, or food, or gossip.

'Five men,' Guthlac said softly. He stood to meet them.

They were coming near, drawn by the fire. They drew close and we heard their footfalls hissing in the frozen grass. And a clink of iron, faint in the darkness.

Guthlac spoke softly. 'Take my bag. Hide!'

The five travellers came boldly, like friends.

'Take my harp too. *Run!*'

I moved away into the shadows. I moved like a weasel. Or a fox in the darkness. I hid Guthlac's leather bag of gold-gifts inside my tunic, and hung the box with his harp on my shoulder. The gold-hoard was small and light. The harp-box hindered my running.

Inside the wood there was a tree, leaning with age. Its boughs were steps rising into the stars. I hid the bag and the harp in undergrowth, and climbed.

Girls do not climb trees in midwinter woods. I was a girl-woman in a boy's clothes.

I heard their words, in greeting, Guthlac and the strangers. Then Guthlac grunted. I looked back from the high tree and saw him in the light of the fire. His tall body bent at the knees and at the waist. Guthlac fell, his life-blood gushed from his throat, and his spirit fled to its long home. I saw Guthlac, the brave minstrel, cut down by thieves.

He was an old man. I heard his death-ghost whisper as it passed over me on its way.

They searched among the cooking pots, seeking gold-hoard. They spoke in anger, finding nothing. 'There was a boy! He had a boy!'

My grass-marks were clear in the hoar-frost. They saw my foot-prints, running to the trees. In my fear I knew that when the story-teller reaches his end the story goes on.

I was the story.

I jumped down from the stair-tree. I grabbed the gift-bag and the harp in its box, and ran in the darkness. There was a chase, ruthless and deadly, in the leafless winter wood. Twigs snapped and dead frozen leaves rustled at my feet. I could not run quietly. We crashed through the trees, the boy-woman in flight, the robber-killers in chase. Guthlac's harp swung and thumped on my back, and the wires twanged quietly inside its box. Breath rasped and heart hammered. Fear filled me. I tripped, I fell, low branches whipped my face.

I was not fast enough.

I heard them following, cruel and bloody, the five thieves who had murdered Guthlac, crashing through trees. Their blood was up. They had murder in their hands. They thought I was a boy.

They were behind me, breathing hard, with sharp knives drawn.

2

ANOTHER TIME

A boy awakens in the warm night.
'Out of bed, quickly!'

With toes on the splintery floorboards and fingers gripping the windowsill, Thomas looks out into the night. Something has disturbed sleep. Someone is out there.

The night swims in full moonlight. From under the brow of the thatch, he looks down into the lane, as if into a pond. On the highest branch of the ash tree that stands on the other side of the lane, a thrush sings every evening at bedtime.

But now, down in the ash tree shadows, there is a concentration of darkness, a bulk of shadow, moving by. A voice is singing quietly. It is not a bird.

Is it a giant?

Hugely tattered, massively shabby, the strange figure lifts from the ground a long, black box, like a child's coffin, and shoulders it. The creature's gigantic head is barely an arm's reach from the watcher's window. *I could snatch off his hat!* Thomas thinks, heart recklessly thumping. *If I dared!*

Does he know I'm watching him?

If he knows, he does not care. With seven-league strides, he climbs the hill and vanishes into moon-darkness.

Back to the mattress Thomas scutters. He clutches the woollen coverlet over his feet, knees, backside and shoulders.

Back to dreams. The giant has walked away with the grey dawn rising around him, but he also strides in the half-light of Thomas's dreams.

What did he have in that box?

*

'Father, there was a giant in the lane during the night.'

'A giant?'

There is uncertainty in the air this morning. Uncertainty in the midsummer sun. Uncertainty in the thick bread, the pale cheese and yesterday's pigeon pie. Even the sky-blue milk jug (Mother's pride and delight) seems to know something secret.

'He was a dream. Your head is full of fancies.'

'No, Mother. He wasn't.'

She frowns. She leans against the sill of the window, pressing her hips. 'A young boy should not,' she says wearily to her husband, 'be allowed to stay with the haymakers until nearly midnight.'

Father looks ashamed.

'It gives them bad dreams.'

'And aches.'

'And blisters,' says Thomas.

'It was no dream,' Father says. 'The giant was real. Like your aches and blisters.'

'Was he a giant?'

'He was a flying stationer.'

'He didn't fly.'

'A walking stationer, then.'

'What is one of them?'

Mother is lowering herself into the rocking chair. 'He's nothing but a common pedlar,' she says.

'He travels round the country selling Banbury books,' Father says. 'I heard he has been at Thaxted and Dunmow. He'll be at Walden Market today.'

'What are Banbury books?'

Mother and Father look at each other. There are memories and secrets.

'What are they?'

'Stories and tales and ballads. They cost a penny each.'

'Do you remember?' says Father.

Mother bursts into joyous laughter.

'What are you laughing at?'

'Something that happened years ago,' Father says. 'Before we had you.'

Thomas is ten years old. He is shut out from their before-they-had-him secrets.

'He must be seven feet tall if he's an inch!' Mother says, thinking back.

'Would you like to go to Walden Market today, Thomas?'

'By myself?'

'Yes.'

'May I buy a Banbury book?'

'Yes. Lots!'

'I've never been by myself. Alone.'

'But you've been with us, often. There's nothing to be afraid of – you're a sensible boy, when you're not daydreaming.'

'It's three miles.' There is a crossroad nearby, with a signpost. It tells travellers they're three miles from Walden.

Thomas thinks and then adds: 'And three miles back.'

'You must take food for the whole day.'

'Can't you come too, Father?'

'No.'

'Because of the haymaking?'

'Yes, Tom. And I want to stay close to home today.'

Strange! The uncertainty in the sunny scullery spreads over the whole countryside.

'How long will it take me?'

'The morning to go. The evening to return. Dare you do it?'

'What must I buy?'

'I'll give you a shilling and some pence. You can buy some Banbury books.'

'*Cock Robin*!' says Mother.

'*Robin Hood*!' says Father.

'And the *Babes in the Wood*.'

Thomas stares and says: 'Who were they?'

'They had no parents, and their wicked uncle didn't want them. He hired some murderers to kill them.'

'Did they die?'

'Yes.'

'Did nobody want them?'

'They loved each other, that's all.'

'It's a terrible, sad tale,' Father says.

'And buy me some sewing scissors at the market,' Mother says. And she says to Father: 'Will he be safe?'

'He's nearly eleven.'

'Will you be here when I get back?' Thomas asks.

'Of course we will, child! What a question!'

3

THIS TIME

Zara is sitting on the edge of her bed, listening to the sun silently singing.

No school this week because of half-term.

Today, she's going into town with her best friend. Dad is coming home in a few days. Mum is downstairs, moving around in the kitchen. She can hear her.

These are the people Zara trusts. Mum, Dad and Rob. She talks to them.

She wriggles her brown toes and thinks how nice her new pale-blue pyjamas are.

Time to get dressed. But first, she pulls back her curtains and looks out into a sky-blue morning in early May, where the birds are shining and busy, and the wallflowers have been patiently growing all through the chilly night in the narrow front garden.

On Zara's window ledge there is:

- ~ an old Barbie doll that once belonged to Mum;
- ~ three ancient clay marbles which Dad dug up in the back garden;
- ~ a leather purse with Euro coins;
- ~ and seven flat, coloured stones.

One of the stones is round, yellow, like an eye looking at her. Zara is sure it's an eye, but she can't tell what kind of eye it is – whether it belongs to an animal, a fish or a bird. Or a magical creature, a dragon perhaps.

She's not sure how she knows it's an eye, but she's certain it is. If she's right, it's not where it's meant to be. It should be fixed in a head of some kind.

On the highest branch of the ash tree on the other side of the lane, there is a thrush, singing its heart out. It composes, waits, performs another few bars, repeats them faultlessly and pauses for applause. *Or for breath*, Zara thinks. *It must breathe sometimes.* Then it starts again. Variations on a theme, this time.

It was doing that when Zara went to bed. She'd sat at her window then too, listening, until she could no longer see the bird in the dark.

But it was still there, singing under the stars.

Night after night, the thrush sings into the deepening dusk, and night after night, Zara plans to stay awake. She wants to know if the thrush sings all through the long midnight and is still singing in the morning, on the other side of darkness. But she always falls asleep, so she still doesn't know.

She rearranges the flat stones on the sill. They were

found many summers ago, when a rubber ball rolled under the radiator pipe, and her searching fingers found the seven dusty bits of stone, slipped down between two uneven floorboards.

Where had they come from? What were they? Who put them there?

They could be Roman, Dad said.

She'd cleaned them up and made a museum. She put a notice on her bedroom door saying: "ENTRANCE FEE 50P", and she quickly collected £3.50. All her family visited and paid. Dad made two visits and was made to pay twice. He'd grumbled about that.

I was in primary school then, she thinks.

Mr Waller couldn't get up their narrow staircase, she recalls. So, the museum was brought downstairs, into the kitchen, so that he could see it there. He paid his 50p without grumbling.

Rob was her assistant museum keeper. He's always been Zara's best friend. He was in primary school too, at that time. In the same class.

Mum and Dad and Rob. The people Zara talks to.

Rob donated a number of the exhibits. A blackbird's nest, some fragments of birds' eggs, a rabbit's skull, a stone with a hole in it, two Victorian pennies and an ancient rolling-pin which once belonged to a long-ago great-great-grandmother. Everything is neatly labelled. The stone with a hole in it has a helpful label saying, "stone with a hole in it".

Zara's phone grunts to tell her there's a message. She leaps up, dives across her bed and belly-flops onto it, stretching frantically over to her dressing table. There is a message from Rob. *Mum's taking us into town. Be here by ten.*

She always feels the tug of companionship when Rob sends her a text. He lives at Rose Farm, a mile away, on the road to Walden. Seeing each other every day is not enough. They have to message each other too.

Zara used to think there was a tubular filament connecting their phones, invisible to all eyes. Along this tube they transmitted tiny words and letters, from one phone to the other. No one else was allowed to use the tube.

She's older now, so she understands the science – approximately – and she knows there is no tiny invisible tube. Not really. But the world is not only the way it is. It's also the way we think about it.

*

'Dad texted,' Mum says. 'He's coming home on Thursday.'

Zara and her Mum are in the sunlit kitchen, seated at the table, facing each other across the packet of muesli, the milk, the toast, the marmalade, the mug of coffee. Mum's ageing laptop lies open at the end of the table, waiting for her to begin her work.

'Can I read it?' Zara bounces dangerously from one chair to the next, with the grace of a hippo. At Mum's laptop she reads: *Hi, long-lost family! I'm expecting to come home on Thursday. Hurrah!!! I'll phone you as soon as I know. Can you meet me at the station, please? Hug you both! XX PS I've missed you.*

There are two kisses, one for each of them. There ought to have been three, but Dad doesn't know that yet.

4

THE FIRST TIME

I was a girl-woman.

Through the wood they followed me, the five men. I ran out, into the meadow on the other side. There was a ditch and a low earth-wall. It was dry and overgrown with dead grasses and kecksies. I hid there, crouching, listening, watching for the five killers.

I stared back into the dark, towards the wood. Holding my breath, I heard another breath, beside me.

Two breathings, side by side. A thigh moved against my thigh, a hip against my hip, a shoulder to my shoulder. A Roman spirit of the night, close by my arm, beside me! In the dry ditch, with me. My heart blood pounded in my chest and thundered in my head. Fear crawled over my skin.

'Come! We must hurry.' It was a whisper, soft and close.

It was a girl's voice, the dead ghost speaking. She took my arm, held my wrist. 'Come!' she said. But her hand was cold on my skin. It was a girl's hand, not a ghost's.

We rose to our feet and stood clear in the starlight. The Guthlac-killers came out of the trees and saw us. They shouted, loud in the night-time. The ghost girl held my arm and ran with me, down to the black stream. Again, it bit my feet. We ran through the shallow water and over the frozen grass.

I cared nothing for bitten toes, for feet in freezing water. The men raced after us, I could hear their breathing. I heard them splash across the stream.

The spirit girl led me towards the stone ruin, the haunt of giants, home of unseen Roman ghosts. Fear gripped me and I broke free of her grasp. 'We must not go in there,' I said.

I stood stock-still. My feet felt the earth, hard and cold.

'You are a girl,' she answered. 'We are both in danger. But we will be safe inside. The men are frit.'

She knew I was not a boy.

Her words were my words, but she spoke them like an outsider. She was not a spirit, she was a girl from another tribe. Or one of the old ones.

'My name is Juliana,' she said.

The robber killers crossed the stream. They shouted, drawing near us. I was breathless and frightened. Juliana led me into the ruin. She pulled me in, fearing to hear the breath of monsters. Inside, we crouched behind a cold wall and watched.

'What is your name?'

'Sæwara.'

Sæwara and Juliana, one woman and one girl. One was frightened, the other was not.

The killers drew near, slowly. They were watchful. They stood side by side, proud like worthy battle comrades, heroes in war, with their weapons drawn. But they were not heroes. They were thieves, killers of old men.

'They will not come in here,' Juliana said. 'They are afeard.' I, Sæwara, was frightened too. But Juliana was calm, a brave battle friend.

The robbers waited a long time. They walked all round the ruin in the frosty starlight, slowly. They dared not come close. We were ghosts who had gone back to the lost times.

One of the five, a bold and reckless leader, walked across the grass and drew near to the Roman walls. His knife blade gleamed in the cold starlight. In his other hand he held Guthlac's cloak, with its golden brooch.

Juliana raised her fists to her mouth and hooted a sound, low and hollow, like the chill voice of the dead, a cry rising from the grave. Three times she hooted.

Then all five thieves fled, the brave killers. At the edge of the wood, one stopped and looked back, their leader, keener than his fellows and more reckless. Then he too vanished among the trees.

Juliana took my hand and led me deeper inside the fallen walls.

*

Inside the big Roman ruin there was a small Saxon half-house, backed against a high stone wall. It was built of wattle and daub. The roof reached down to the ground. It was made of grey thatch tied in bundles. Moss grew on the thatch, small hills of green. The house was old. The door was like a brock hole. On hands and knees, I followed Juliana inside.

She took two sticks and made fire. Juliana's spirits helped her, and the fire came quickly. As she crouched over the sticks, the first flame came as bright as a bee. She pushed it into dried grass and twigs.

Guthlac used to say that an open-air fire would cook for you but would not warm you. He said the sky was huge and hungry and would swallow up the heat. But Juliana's fire was under her roof, out of the sky's cold reach.

She had a great bundle of animal skin, rolled into a ball. She wedged this into the door-hole to shut out the night cold.

Side by side we sat for warmth, wrapped in skins, with a stone wall at our backs. It was a Roman wall, but there were no dead Roman spirits.

Why had the mad Romans built stone houses without roofs? Who had built a small Saxon house, against a wall, inside the big Roman house?

Juliana gave me bread. We ate our supper crouched over the fire. Its light flickered the shadows. Wood-smoke filled the small roof space over our heads and threaded its way through the thatch. Outside, the freezing stars shone in the winter night.

I thought of Guthlac, frozen on the hard earth, unburied.

'I knew Guthlac,' Juliana said. 'He was a brave man, a wayfarer, a song-singer for warriors. He played his harp and told me stories. I gave him food. He came at midday; we ate at sunset. In the morning he went away.'

She spoke like the field slaves at my homestead. Her words were mostly my words, but some were like strangers.

I told her about the great hall of King Rædwald, the sea king, the overlord, giver of gold to all his followers. But she knew nothing of the king, the sea warrior. The sea was a dream to her.

'I have seen the sea,' I told her.

She took my hand, and we went outside. The stars were bitter and sharp in the black sky.

She took me round the Roman ruin. Round and back to where we started. I tripped and fell on fallen stones, half-buried in the dank winter grass.

Juliana knew every stone, every hollow.

She looked out into the night, into the trees, into the shadows. A fox barked. There was no other sound in the frosty darkness.

The five robber murderers had gone away. 'We are safe,' she said to me.

Until daylight, I thought.

Then Juliana showed me a wonder. She carried a burning branch and led me to a roofless stone place. It was inside the Roman house but open to the naked, freezing sky.

There was a flat floor. With her bare foot, she swept away dead leaves and dirt. In the flame-light I saw a bird, flat on the ground, bright and glowing. The air around it was white. I crouched down and felt cold stone. The bird's body was blue, and its legs were red. Its tail was long; its neck was stooped; its feathers shone.

A floor likeness! Made of stones, flat and bright. I had never seen such a thing. Only a god could have put it there, in that place.

In the flickering flame shadows, the bird moved, as if for flight.

But it had no eye, only a hole in the flatness. A bird, bright and sightless.

Juliana held my hand. 'One day the bird will fly away,' she said. 'But first it must get back its eye. Then it will sing and fly home.'

Back at her fireside, we snugged together under thick animal skins. She smelled of wood smoke.

We slept with a stone wall behind us and the fire at our feet. It was a hard bed. We lay close for comfort.

5

ANOTHER TIME

A road often travelled on high horseback behind Father is not the same when the traveller is alone, on foot. It has different ups, different downs and steeper banks. Hedges are higher. Landmarks are not true to memory.

This is the road to all of England, Thomas thinks. I am a Banbury bookseller, seven feet high and afraid of nobody! I am journeying over all of England. First, I will go to Cambridge, then to Newmarket, then to Timbuktu, then to Thaxted, then to London Town and then back to Banbury Cross for more Banbury books.

But what *is* a Banbury book? At home there is a prayer book, a bible, a *Pilgrim's Progress* and *Robinson Crusoe*. What is so special about Banbury books?

Uncle William leans over his hedge and wants to know where the traveller is going.

'I'm going to Walden market.'

'Never!'

'Yes, I am.'

'It's about time you stretched your legs,' says Uncle William.

'Is Aunt Meg going haymaking?'

'Not today, child. She is off to your house to be with your mother.'

More secrets and mysteries.

Uncle William advises the short way through Howe's Wood. 'Take the old grass road,' he says, 'and straight on by the mossy milestone. There's nothing to be afeared of.'

But Thomas is a wise boy, and he knows better than to take advice from an uncle who sends a child alone into a wood.

So he stays on the road.

*

Later, there's a whiskery brown man layering a hedge. He climbs out from a tangle of brambles and branches and waits in the road, facing the young traveller.

'Where be you going to this fine midsummer morning?'

'To market, sir.'

'To market, to market, to buy a fat pig?'

Thomas thinks this is foolish.

'No sir. To buy some Banbury books.'

The hedge weaver pushes back his hat, wipes his brow and travels back to childhood. 'I wouldn't half like to have one of them,' he says. 'For my little girl, y' know.'

He hasn't got a little girl, but better not say anything. Thomas knows he hasn't got a boy either.

'Will you bring me one?'

'Yes.'

'I haven't any money,' says the labourer sadly.

What is to be done then? Thomas stares at the labourer's belt buckle. He is impatient to get on.

'If you're walking all that way, you should have a stout stick to help you over the miles.'

He selects a hazel branch, lops it, trims it and smooths it off. Its knobbly root end is smooth-hewn and shaped to the palm of a boy.

'There! This end is for the road. And this end is for robbers' heads.'

I'm not a small child anymore, Thomas thinks. 'I won't meet any robbers.'

'Have you money?'

'Yes.'

'Then look out for robbers. There's always danger.'

Thomas sighs. He hadn't thought of that.

'You might meet Napoleon Bogeyman! So, you need to watch out! A big stick in exchange for a small book.'

This is nonsense too, but Thomas ignores it. 'What story shall I buy for you?'

'Something with a bit of bawdy in it.'

'What's bawdy?'

'Ask the Banbury man. He'll have something.'

'Will your daughter like the bawdy?'

'Ah, well!'

'Will you be here when I get back?'

'No, I won't. See! In that gatepost, where there's a crack in the wood, poke the book inside that! And I'll find it.'

'This stick will be too small when I grow up.'

'It will grow with you. Didn't you know that? All my walking sticks grow.'

Thomas knows that's a joke, but it is a good stick. He is taller with its companionship. But it must be hidden outside the town, he thinks, for fear of mockery. Or robbers.

*

Outside Rose Farm, an old man sits in a wooden chair, with a bowl of early potatoes on his bony knees and a scraping knife in his hand. His face is long and lopsided, with a bleary-leary eye.

Children are scared of Old Lopsy. He is in their dreams, their games, their stories. Looking at his old head nodding innocently among the cow parsley, with the pond behind him, you would never guess how fierce he can be! He *hates* young boys! He ignores girls; he tenderly loves his cats; he is kind to his dog; he is good with cows and sheep; and he used to have a way with the big farm horses, but boys fill him with rage.

And he is fast, too, on those skinny shanks.

How to get past? Run for it? Stride bravely by and hope not to be noticed?

Mother says Old Lopsy is as mad as a grasshopper, but Father says he is just angry.

He is angry enough today! The sight of a boy walking

in the sunshine past his house throws him into a fury. He shouts; he spits; he swears; and his poor, twisted face shakes with rage.

'Cheeky young ruffian!' (Thomas has not said a word!) 'I'll show you! I'll twist your bloody head off!'

A young woman runs from the back of the farm, with apron strings flying, waving a wooden rolling-pin.

Old Lopsy hurls the potatoes, scraping knife and the tin bowl at the innocent passer-by.

'French spy! Get you back to Ole Boney!'

The young woman is angry. 'Granddad! They were the first early taters of the year!'

Old Lopsy gives her a humble look of shame and forgets about French spies.

Pelleted and stung, Thomas stoops to gather up the potatoes. With the spuds, there are some stones. They are strange, with one flat side, coloured blue or red. One stone is yellow, and round. He cradles them all in his hands, held like a bowl against his stomach.

Old Lopsy's granddaughter crosses the lane to take the rescued potatoes. 'Thanks,' she says to Thomas.

'What about the stones?' he says to her.

'You can keep them,' she says. 'He keeps on finding them. All over the place!'

Thomas slips the flat, coloured stones into a pocket, with his money.

Seven of them.

'He means no harm. He wouldn't have hurt you.'

But Thomas is not so sure. He continues on his journey. There is still a long way to go.

6

THIS TIME

Every morning Zara and her mum talk over breakfast. Sometimes their words drift lazily from one to the other like wisps of candle smoke, softly, hardly bothering to find their way. At other times they are fired like bullets, aimed, and so quick and sharp that a listener would be confused. Sometimes they make long, thoughtful sentences, curving gracefully across the table in an elegant ballet of words and meanings.

This daily breakfast talk with Mum is essential. Even on school mornings, when there's little time.

But with other people, Zara is tongue-tied, word-locked. "Yes" and "thank you" are sometimes brave enough to slip quietly into the open. But the other words in her head are shy and refuse to come out. She has thousands of them, all waiting to be used.

She'll grow out of it, people say. But she hasn't.

'Will Dad be tired when he gets here?' she says.

'I don't know about *tired* – he'll be *fed up*, that's for sure! But he'll be pleased to be coming home!'

Dad has been away for more than a month. He has been to North Africa because his father died. He's had to visit his brothers and sisters and all his aunts and uncles and cousins. And he helped to arrange his father's funeral. *I expect he had to do a lot of talking with all those people,* Zara thinks.

'Will he be very sad?'

'Yes, of course. His dada has died, so he will be sad.'

I'll be very sad when my mum and dad die, Zara thinks happily. She feels proud of how sad she'll be when that day comes.

'But we have a secret to tell him,' she says.

Zara's mum is pregnant, but this was not confirmed until after Dad had left. So he knows nothing about it. It's their secret to tell.

'Can I tell Rob?'

'Yes. But Dad should be told first. *Then* Rob.'

Sometimes when Mum has a shower, Zara goes into the bathroom to examine her stomach. They are not embarrassed about this. But there are no signs yet. Zara, however, is not worried by this lack because she has a teenager's understanding of baby-making. 'The baby will grow,' she says. 'Then you'll get fat.'

They are playing games; they often do that.

'Thanks for explaining that,' Mum says. 'It's good to know.'

The baby is like the words in Zara's head. It won't come out until it's ready.

But the words come out fast enough at breakfast! Talk, talk, talk! Non-stop.

There is a knock on the door. It's old Mr Waller who lives in the house on the other side of the lane. He owns the big wood that starts at the end of his back garden. And the ash tree in his front garden, where the thrush sings.

But he doesn't own the thrush, Zara thinks. The thrush belongs to itself.

Zara stops talking. With Mr Waller she is silent. Her sentences are queuing up inside her head, waiting until he's gone. This makes her feel invisible. And sad. But she can't help it.

While she's busy not saying anything, her phone grunts again. It's another text from Rob. *I have something for you.*

His words and letters have reached the end of their journey along the secret invisible tube. Zara imagines them racing and tumbling over one another in their eagerness to get to her. Like tiny comical animals in a Disney film. But, in spite of their excitement, they always arrive in the right order. It's a miracle.

And yet she knows perfectly well there is no tube and no words racing headlong to get to her.

Mr Waller – having asked about Dad – has left. Mum has cleared away the breakfast things, and Zara has stacked the dishes in the dishwasher.

'Are you going to Rob's this morning?'

'Yes. His mum is taking us into Walden.'

'To the auction?'

'I expect so,' Zara says hopefully. Rob's mum likes antiques, and she always goes to the monthly auction sale.

'I expect you'll be taking your £20 then,' Mum says. 'Just in case.'

'Of course I will,' Zara says. She usually takes a £20 note when she goes shopping. The same £20 note, every time. She never buys anything unless someone is with her to make the purchase, usually Rob.

'Don't forget to say thank you to Rob's mum.'

Zara promises. She knows the word will come out so quietly that Rob's mum probably won't hear it. But she never criticises or grumbles because she knows Zara is thinking *thank you* even if she's not saying it.

Zara is troubled by having to talk to people. Knowing that someone is listening to her, attending to what she says, is just as bad. Her mum and dad and Rob are the only exceptions. And sometimes her English teacher.

She likes *them* to pay attention, but for the rest of the world, her tongue is tied.

And she feels invisible.

7

THE FIRST TIME

Sleep would not come. Memory visited me and my mind flashed back.

I remembered a straight road, white and stony. Men said it was built by the mad Roman gods. It bypasses our homestead and our fields. It is cut like a battle scar from the south sky to the north sky. No one walks on the empty, straight road. Only the grasses grow there. People who cross must leap over, like deer.

When I was young, I played jumping games on the Roman road, with Eadweard. We squealed if our feet touched the highway. We were frightened of the Romans, who were mad with magic and power. On midsummer nights, we walked along the road, fearing unseen ghosts, in flying carts or riding on horses. They would reach down and sweep us up in their arms and take us away to Rome.

But all we found there was the fear in our hearts. We were young, we ran home in the darkness, holding hands.

Why did they go away, the Roman giants? They left no stories across the generations, only roofless castles falling into ruin and roads like whip scars on the bare backs of the hills.

Eadweard and I hurried back to the village as darkness fell. Our houses were made of wood and thatch and dried mud. They were shaped for round buttocks and stooping shoulders. And our paths are not straight like whiplashes. They follow streams and hillsides and the edges of woods.

Once, after dark, Eadweard and I saw a dead Roman hand rising from the road-stones to grab us by the heels and take us to the lower world. Or to Rome. We gasped in fear and ran away. Afterwards, I went back, and the dead hand had turned into a mushroom. Eadweard called me Sæwara the Fearless.

Eadweard was my child friend. My trust companion.

*

Then Guthlac came and took me with him. He took me from the great hall, and he shouted at me. 'You must become a boy!' he shouted. 'Girls are always in danger. You must be a boy!'

'Then take a boy!' I said. 'If you want a boy, take one!' He was old and tall, like a man-tree. But I was not afraid of him.

In spite of my anger, my heart longed to go with him,

to walk with Guthlac across the empty country to the hall of the king in the east, King Rædwald, the sea warrior. So I became a boy – I wore a boy's woollen clothes – and I left the hall of my kinsfolk to go with Guthlac.

Eadweard gave me his knife. He grieved in his heart at my going.

'Listen!' Guthlac ordered as we went our way. 'And learn!' He shouted his list of kings and queens.

King Wuffa and his son Tytila.
Ethelfrit, killed in battle by King Rædwald.
Edwin of Deira, Rædwald's godson.
Queen Clothilde and Queen Sigewise,
and Sæwara, a young princess, your namesake...

We walked a mile. Then he said, 'Give me back my list of kings and queens.'

I told him every king, every queen and every princess.

...and Sæwara, a young princess, my namesake.

I was a story-teller. Guthlac grunted. It was his way.

*

But with Guthlac, there were no leaping games in the winter twilight. Eadweard, my child companion, was not with me.

Now Guthlac was dead. My thoughts were full of memories of him.

He always cooked at duskfall. But there was no cooking in his stories, no slaughtering of pigs, no gutting of dead rabbits or gathering of berries. No grinding of flour or baking of bread, no skinning of onions. No backache, no sore hands or weeping eyes.

Yet he always cooked, every day, as darkness fell.

There had been smoke from a fire when I went back to him that day as the winter light faded. His long body bent over the pot. We ate roast chicken legs that night, with leeks. And hard cheese.

We did not know it was Guthlac's last meal. No man can know what is to come.

'We will be home in two days,' he said. His big body crouched in the shadows. His eyes shone in the firelight.

His leather bag was beside him, holding his treasures. A few gold rings, some brooches, clasps and precious necklets. They were gifts from kings and chieftains, tributes for storytelling. 'All great men give gifts of love and honour,' Guthlac said. 'That is the way to win the loyalty of brave men and women.'

He said those things every day.

Questions troubled me. 'Why did you take me from the hall of my people?' I said. 'There were boys, lots of boys! Boys are eager for danger! Why did you choose a girl of sixteen years to take to the hall of the sea king?'

The darkness pressed around us. The fire crackled softly. The frost was keen. A thin moon slid behind the distant hills, like half a yellow bracelet in the sky.

Guthlac chewed slowly, swallowed, and spoke.

'The boys have no stories,' Guthlac said. His words

were bitter. 'They are born to be warrior meat! But you are a word-weaver. You are a story-storer, a song-singer.'

'I will be a mother,' I said. 'All mothers are song-singers and story-tellers.'

I thought those words would make him angry. His voice was grim. 'All the brave heroes will need your songs and stories,' he said. 'The leaders of men will reward you with treasure and honour you. You will hold the people together.'

Guthlac talked like that. It was his way.

So I put on the clothes of a boy, and I left the hall of my kinsmen and went with Guthlac. I had to be a boy-girl, for safety. No one must see, no one must know. So I taught myself to walk like a boy, climb like a boy, and piss like a boy.

As we walked through woods and heaths and meadows, Guthlac told me stories of dragon-worms, of great kings and their warriors, of the rise and fall of brave leaders, givers of golden gifts. And of ice-cold journeys across the grey sea.

But he told no stories going uphill. He saved his breath for walking.

'There are no stories here,' he said. 'Only the ones we brought when we came in boats over the grey whale-road. This country is empty. We brought our words and our gods. Our stories hold everything,' he said.

Then I argued with him. 'But there is danger here, there are battles here! Where there are battles, there must be stories!'

'But no heroes,' he shouted. 'There are no heroes!' His

voice was bitter. With the sadness on him, he said again: 'There are no brave fighters, only small men and small women.'

Guthlac was wrapped in tales of battle heroes of long ago. His tales were forged in the old countries. They sailed with our people in boats across the grey sea. They told of brave men and fierce women, cruel storms and bitter winters. And they told of lonely exiles, without friends and without kin. All our stories looked back in longing to the old lost countries.

But I am young. This land is my land. Its mild woods and pale skies, its low hills and its green, winding pathways, belong to me. My land is full of wonders and new people. And King Rædwald.

I thought of Eadweard, my child friend, my boy companion since the first light of day shone into our eyes. We are young, in a young country, full of eager joy in hall and field.

Eadweard was a boy. I was a girl. I made a song for him.

We took honey from the hives and were stung bitterly.
We carried bundles of reeds for thatch, and our skin
    was sore and torn.
We played with the king's dogs and were bitten.
We helped in the mill and Eadweard crushed his
    finger.
We swam in the river and caught eels in the fish weir.
We lay on the dusty earth under the oak floor of
    the hall,

listening, secret and hidden, with bright eyes.
Through a crack in the boards, Wulfstan the reeve
saw us and had us whipped.

I slept at last, thinking of Eadweard.

*

Juliana woke as the darkness paled. We talked. Time passed.

My heart wept for Guthlac. I opened the wooden box. Its hinges and its latch were made by Wilferth, our ironsmith. Inside, the harp lay in soft beaver skin, nestling.

Guthlac called it Joy-Giver.

'Can you make it sing?' Juliana asked.

'The harp is Guthlac's,' I said. 'I do not know its craft.'

I held the harp as a mother holds her baby. It was hard and honey-hued, smooth where Guthlac's touch had worn it. There were six strings made of horse-hair and six pegs made of bone.

In the cold dawn light, I lightly touched each string. There was a thin dream of song-craft. Guthlac said he would teach me.

Juliana said: 'Perhaps the Joy-Giver will teach you.'

8

THIS TIME

Professor Molly Barnes is an archaeologist. She knows a great deal about the past, the Anglo-Saxon past especially. Someone recently, introducing her to an audience, said she was a kind of time traveller. Privately, she regards this notion as foolish.

But in spite of that, she has recently started to have dreams of *her own* past, her personal story. Events, episodes and sequences from her early years have started to come back to her. Not as sleeping dreams and mostly not archaeological. They arrive when she's just waking up in the morning or dozing in the afternoon sun. There's nothing confusing or arbitrary about them. Nothing dreamlike at all. And they're not just brief, fragmentary images, loosely connected.

No. They are full-on compilations of lost memories, assembling themselves into narratives and coming back to her with a bright and vivid immediacy that compels attention.

As if she's excavating her own history. Or it's excavating itself, before her half-sleeping eyes. More than eighty years of it.

*

She recalls a warm summer night during the war, when Adam was in hospital. He'd been knocked unconscious and badly concussed in an explosion. *I was eleven years old,* she recalls. Adam too.

At around an hour before midnight, Molly got out of bed and put on shorts, shirt and sandals.

The house was sleeping. Quietly, she opened her bedroom door and walked cautiously along the passage and down the stairs. Quietly into the kitchen she went, and quietly she raided the contents of the larder. Her thieving was modest and would hopefully pass unnoticed – nothing more than half a pork pie, two slices of ham and six digestive biscuits.

Can I really remember all this? she thinks. *Or am I making it up?* One by one, in orderly succession, the details are uncovered and reveal themselves.

In the backyard, she stood still for a moment, checking there were no twitching curtains, no one watching from an upstairs window. Then she went for her bike. She put the pie, the ham and the biscuits into the saddlebag, where she'd already stowed two bars of chocolate.

She's an academic, so she checks herself momentarily,

in search of an editorial mistake. But this dream (if that's what it is) is correct: chocolate had not yet been rationed.

She wheeled the bike to the road, mounted and set off, relishing the night air. It was flowing like cool water through the empty silent streets, she recalls. She could see clearly because there was a bright half-moon. It was around midsummer and the nights were short.

There were no cars, no street lights. Nothing but silence. As she cycled clear of the last houses and out into the open country, she thought of the ARP watchers on the church tower and wondered if they could see her moving like a shadow along the empty road.

It would have taken me about an hour to get to Ely, she thinks. She feels an old woman's envy, longing for the energy of the young. She'd cycled steadily, not allowing herself to get out of breath. *Was I nervous, out on my own in the middle of the night?* But no, she wasn't! At that age, she was rarely certain enough about anything to be really determined, but when she made up her mind, she was fearless and resolute.

After five miles of cycling, she reached Littleport, empty and still. Through the town she went, taking a side street to avoid the police station and keeping well away from the church – here too they would have their air-raid wardens on duty.

Eventually, she came to the outskirts of Ely, where the RAF Hospital was.

Here she knew she had to be more cautious. The main gate was open and unguarded, and Molly dismounted and wheeled her bike inside the grounds. She left it in some bushes and set off on foot towards the hospital entrance. She remembers unbuckling the saddlebag with its stiff leather straps, clutching it, scuttling from tree to tree, from shrub to shrub, staying parallel to the main drive on her right.

At the front entrance of the main building, a guard stood at ease, in dark-blue uniform, with his rifle resting on its butt on the ground beside him.

Molly crouched and waited, hoping he would move away. But instead, she heard the sound of marching footfalls, and two more guards came round the corner and approached the entrance. One of them was a sergeant; his white stripes were luminous in the moonlight.

'Left, right, left, right. Halt!' Steel-tipped heels clacked crisply in unison.

The guard was being changed. Molly heard more commands – 'Fall in!' and 'Fall out!' One guard was being relieved, and another took his place. In less than a minute, there was silence again. She could hear the marching steps growing fainter round the back of the building. The new guard stood just as still and attentive as the first one had done. The relieved guard would, she supposed, have a few hours' sleep.

She waited, crouching, sweating, irritated by twigs and spiders' webs touching her face. When she could bear it no longer, she found a large clump of dry earth and lobbed it high into the bushes on the other side of the drive.

Its landing was a slightly whispered clatter as it fell through the leaves, and the guard was instantly alert. Molly watched. It took a second throw – a large stone this time – to convince the airman that he'd better leave his post and investigate.

While he was poking around in the bushes, Molly legged it across the space and round the corner and into the big, shadowy garden at the side of the hospital. There was no money in wartime to spend on planting flowers, but the grass was kept mown and the big island beds were full of overgrown shrubs. She moved unseen from shadow to shadow towards the wall of the building, close to Adam's ward.

There was a side entrance. She'd taken note of it during her afternoon's visit, with the others. And there was another man on guard, but this one must have been given orders to patrol from place to place. He threw away an illicit cigarette, hoisted his rifle onto his shoulder and set off towards the back of the hospital building.

Molly ran to the door and pushed.

She moved stealthily along a corridor and came to a place she recognised – a small office with glass windows – and inside, a duty nurse working at her desk. Because it was an RAF hospital, she was a sergeant. Molly ducked low and crept into the ward unseen, clutching the saddlebag close to her chest.

She remembers the smell of mustiness and disinfectant and feeling sharply aware that she was in a room full of *men*: men sleeping and dreaming, recovering from sickness and injury, silent except for their night breathing. Two of them were snoring loudly. For the first time, she was frightened. One of the patients – who sat upright and staring all through visiting hours – was still sitting up now, with his eyes wide open. She was expecting him to shout out and raise the alarm. But his eyes stared unseeing as she crept past the end of his bed.

When she reached Adam, she ducked down and tapped his shoulder to waken him. But he didn't stir. She leaned in close and whispered his name into his ear. That didn't work either. So she pulled the bed covers off. She sometimes did that at home, when he wouldn't get up in the mornings.

He opened his eyes and looked uncertainly at her. 'Hello,' he whispered, just as if he'd been waiting for her. Sleepily, he raised himself onto one elbow and nodded. *Why did he nod like that?*

'Is there somewhere we can go?' Molly whispered. 'I can't stay here!'

Immediately Adam was fully awake. Between his bed and the next was a window, left slightly open for fresh air. Adam – checking first that the duty nurse in her glass office was not watching – opened the window more widely. It was one of those metal-frame windows which always creaked, Molly remembers. But, miraculously, this one opened soundlessly, and in an instant, Adam was astride the sill and then jumping down outside.

Molly followed. She remembers reaching back inside and pulling the curtains across.

'This way!' Adam said. And then: 'Why have you come?'

'I'm going to tell you what happened.'

We rarely wasted words, she thinks. 'About time someone did!' Adam said.

The doctor's ruling for visitors was that no mention should be made about the night of the explosion. Adam had been badly concussed, and it would confuse him. There could be a serious setback to his recovery.

But Molly knew better. Adam was not traumatised, just frustrated and angry at not being told.

He led Molly to a narrow brick path between overgrown island beds of thick, abundant growth. *Supposing he dies,* Molly thought, *now, while he's with me. It will be my fault!*

But she knew he wouldn't.

Did I really think that? Or have I just made it up? She knows memory is a creative process, not just documentary.

He led her to a grassy clearing where there was a large, circular pond with a low brick wall. In the middle was a fountain, switched off every night. But the pond was full and deep, the water cool and inviting.

The cycle ride had made Molly hot and sweaty. 'Let's have a dip,' Adam said. He stripped off his pyjamas and lowered himself into the water, and Molly followed suit ('Aaah! Oooh!'). She suspected Adam had done this before, but she doesn't remember asking him.

Am I speculating about this now? she asks herself. *Or did I wonder about it* then? When did the questioning take place? Who – and where – is the editor in charge of all this remembering? Who is in charge of this dig?

Afterwards, shivering, they put their things back on and sat side by side in the summer darkness with their feet in the water, stretching and waggling their toes.

This is heaven! Molly thought. *Wicked forbidden*

heaven! And then she thought: *suppose there's an air raid. Mum will find out I'm not in my bedroom.*

They shared the pork pie, the ham slices and the biscuits, she recalls. Then they turned round and sat with their backs against the wall of the pond, and that's when she started to tell him what had happened on the night of the explosion.

She'd thought about it a lot, working out in advance what he would most want to know. But what a listener wants to know is rarely the same as what the teller wants to tell. So there were interruptions and questions. Then Adam needed some parts to be told a second time, or in more detail. Or more slowly so that he could savour it.

Her version was a draft, improvised and disorderly; with his collaboration, it became a story.

They were there for almost two hours, though to Molly it seemed like twenty minutes. And when at last they'd done – and when Adam's amazement and admiration had calmed a little – Molly produced the two bars of chocolate.

Dessert.

Neither of them had a watch. 'I'd better go,' Molly said. *But I didn't want to leave. I wanted to stay there.*

Adam insisted on accompanying her to where she'd left her bike. 'I want to be sure you don't get caught,' he said. But Molly wanted to see him back to the ward for the same reason. 'But no,' he said – anyone who saw him out at night would just assume he was sleepwalking.

'They think I'm daft anyway.'

There was still a sentry at the main entrance by the road. He heard their movements and instantly shouted,

'Who goes there?' In the quiet of the night, they heard a sinister click as he slipped off the safety catch of his .303.

'Run!' Adam whispered to Molly.

And as she disappeared into the shadows, he stepped out onto the drive, clearly visible in his pyjamas and his white head-bandage bright in the darkness.

'What the bloody..?'

The guard had raised his rifle. 'Christ! I thought you were a spy! You come with me, you young scallywag! You'll be for the high jump when Matron hears about this.'

Molly heard what he said. Matron was also a sergeant major. But Adam would care nothing for her wrath.

As she set off towards home on her bike, she saw that the north-east sky ahead of her was already growing lighter. She began to sing "Daisy Bell" softly. But she put different words to the tune. *Molly, Molly! Tell me the story, do!*

He'll be all right now, she thought.

The tyres of her bike hissed softly on the road, and when she was safely out in the flat, empty countryside, she began to sing – loudly, joyously, triumphantly.

She wonders how much of this memory she can trust. It has the vividness of a lucid dream. And it's been happening a lot lately – dreams that come to her with a powerful and authoritative narrative coherence.

They won't be denied.

I sang – on and off – all the way home, she thinks.

9

THIS TIME

'Phone me when you get to Rob's house,' Mum says.

Zara protests. 'But I'll be there in five minutes! I'm not an *infant*!'

'Never mind! Phone! I like to know you're safe.' They have this conversation every time. Almost exactly the same words, in almost exactly the same order.

Zara's house is at the bottom of a hill. The hill is steep, and she has to begin her cycling with a standing start. Mum watches her set off, then she goes inside.

There is green leaf litter on the road, twig ends and broken bits of branches. An early hedge trimmer has driven along the lane, its blades rattling, searing off last year's growth.

'There's history in a hedge,' her uncle once told her. 'They are hundreds of years old.'

But now the hedge looks torn and hurt, with jagged

ends exposed – hawthorn, maple, elder, bramble. The sky can blow right through it. But it's happened before and Zara knows the hedge will be quickly healed, green and growing again after a couple of weeks.

But the birds are not happy.

From the top of the hill, Zara has a view so wide that its edges fade into the sky a thousand miles away. When she was little, she used to believe you could see the skyscrapers of New York from this hill, or Moscow, but that was before she knew the earth was round. She still half-believes you might be able to see them if only you had a perfectly clear day.

Or if you had an app that would let you see around bends on your phone, a *magiscope* perhaps, or a *bendy app*. She invented one once but only in her mind. If you had one, you would be able to look all the way round the world and see yourself from behind.

Rising from deep in the valley, Walden steeple reassures her that she's on the right road. 'I am higher than you,' she says to it from the top of her hill.

In her mind as she cycles, there is the memory of a cold night in January, when Rob was walking home with her. The wind roared and it started to snow, and within minutes there was a blizzard. She was excited and scared, but they would come to no harm because there were two of them, he said.

That was a good time! When they reached home, Zara's mum said Rob couldn't go back in such weather. A text message settled it, and Rob had a sleepover. For supper, Dad cooked eggs, sausages and chips, with baked beans. That was the sort of supper you needed when you'd been in a blizzard, he said.

Now, Rob will be waiting for her, at the foot of the hill just before the road turns a sharp corner, beside the pond outside Rose Farm.

What's he got for me? she wonders.

From here it is downhill all the way to Rob's house. Joyous, effortless freewheeling, with nothing to do but steer!

There he is! As she knew he would be.

She checks behind her, then cruises across the road to where he is, crouched at the edge of his pond, peering into the water. She comes to a precise stop, neatly and elegantly, right beside him.

'I've got to go to the dentist,' Rob says. He is not complaining for himself. He's preparing Zara for disappointment. 'It won't take long, and I'll meet you afterwards.'

Zara follows him along the edge of the pond, wheeling her bike. A stream flows out of the pond and under the road. In wet weather, it flows over the road too. In the trees at the back of the house, the same stream flows into the pond and keeps it full.

On the far side, there is a thicket of reeds and rushes. Some geese live there, but today they are out in the fields in search of food. Once, she'd plucked up courage to ask Rob's mum where the geese came from.

'They've always been here,' she said. 'As far as I know.'

Rob picks his way across some stepping stones. Zara lays her bike on the grass and follows him over.

The water twinkles cheerfully at her. But the stream doesn't always behave nicely. After heavy rain, it is wild and muddy and restless. It turns over in its bed and changes its position. There is a small, earth cliff, perfect for sitting on with your feet in the water in hot weather. But this paddling seat is not where it was last summer. The stream has moved it, almost a metre.

Today the water is clear, and Zara can see minnows and sticklebacks. If I were tiny, she thinks, no bigger than my thumb, I could swim with them. If Rob were a better swimmer, he could dive in beside me. Zara imagines a perfect dive into transparent water, as clean and smooth as a needle into silk! And all the small, perfect fish would be waiting to greet a tiny, perfect Zara.

And everything would be all right, because fish don't talk, and they wouldn't expect her to say anything.

There is a flat area of fresh grass, kept short by the geese. They feed on it, and they fertilise it. On the grass, waiting for her, is a chunk of old cement, about the size of a saucer.

Rob lays it in the palm of Zara's hand, and she turns it over. It is heavy and ugly. One side is grey and rough, like hardened mud. But embedded in the other side are fifteen flat stones, roughly square. Most of them are apple green. They are like the seven stones in her bedroom, about the same size and thickness and coloured. But these are fixed in the lump of cement.

'You can have it for your museum.'

'Where did you find it?'

'In the stream. I think there might be more. We ought to have a search.'

But there is no time for searching. Rob's mum calls that she's ready to go, and they hurry off to the car.

Doors are slammed, seat belts clicked. Walden, here we come!

*

Zara and Rob have visited the sale room since they were little. They examine the items and make murmured comments about them to each other. They whisper about the buyers too. And the auctioneer.

There is a sale every month. But today Rob has to have his teeth checked at the dentist's, and his mum is going with him. They will meet Zara later. Rob's mum has spoken to the auctioneer's wife, who is a friend of hers. She has asked her to keep an eye on Zara.

Zara is a teenager, so it's probably good that she doesn't know about this. She often feels as if no one ever notices her, and she dislikes it, but she would also hate being especially watched. That would be worse.

Left alone, she is fearful. Someone might speak to her, trapping her in an entanglement of words. She presses back into a corner beside a big mahogany wardrobe and watches the people moving slowly around, stooping, peering, talking quietly.

The big hall is full of objects for sale. There are tables and chairs, cushions and mirrors, wirelesses and whatnots; there are tall statues and small statuettes; there are boxes of books, boxes of cutlery, boxes of jewellery; there are pictures in frames, pictures without frames and frames without pictures.

And moving among them are the buyers and busybodies, the wheelers and dealers, stooping, peering, poking, whispering to one another. And a few onlookers who do nothing but look on.

Someone is watching her. A boy glowers at her from under a dark hood. She supposes he is a boy, but there's no way of being sure. He is tall, skinny, leaning against the back wall. There always seems to be someone watching her, she thinks. She's only recently noticed this. Men usually.

Zara's eyes fall upon an object unlike anything else in the sale room. She is arrested at once, curious and excited, and she edges through the crowd so that she can get close to it.

On a walnut dressing table, between a purple vase and a black marble clock, stands a birdcage. She has never seen a birdcage like it. It's old and round and tall and stands on a circular base. It is rusty and dirty. Inside, on a perch, is a metal bird. It is shabby and disused, but there are signs of long-lost brightness, remains of ancient colour. There are apple-green flecks on the wings, hints of vermillion among the tail feathers and tiny sapphire-blue circles around its sharp black eyes. The small beak is yellow.

Zara has fallen in love. She feels that she has wanted all her life to have this bird. It has come here especially to be found and rescued by her. A need in her has been exactly recognised and provided for. It is a need she didn't know she had, but now she has to live with it.

She must have the sad and shabby bird. It wants her to buy it.

But desire brings rivalry. There is a man in a corduroy jacket, and he too is interested in the little bird in its cage. The man uses his hip to edge Zara out of the way, ignoring her, not even noticing she is there.

She was used to this when she was little; she knew it happened because she was just a child. But she's almost grown up now, and it's still happening. She feels indignant. She has her revenge by eavesdropping, by stealing his words and taking possession of his knowledge.

'What do you think?' the man says to the woman who is with him.

'It's *tat*!' She is contemptuous of the bird in its cage.

Zara feels as if they are talking about her.

'It could be cleaned up.'

'Dare say. But does it work? It's supposed to sing.'

The man picks up the birdcage and finds a metal key in its base, which he winds rustily. *He has horrible fingers*, Zara thinks. There is a small switch which he moves across.

The man and the woman stoop and lean in to hear better. So does Zara, unnoticed. But the only sound is a faint and regular clicking from inside the circular base. Something is alive in there – but only just. A faint mechanical pulse. A small heart, barely able to beat.

Then a miracle! The tiny bird moves. Its head and upper neck are turning hopefully from one side to the other as if in search of something, a rescuer perhaps. And the small yellow beak opens and closes soundlessly.

Silent Zara and silent bird catch each other's eye, and Zara (totally and recklessly in love) knows what she must do. She asks herself if she *can* do it, if she *dares* to do it and if she has enough money to do it. And anyway, are you allowed to make bids at an auction if you're under eighteen?

She can't believe it's possible. But it might be!

The auction begins. Time passes. Zara moves back into her corner and waits anxiously, at a distance, carefully not looking at the bird in its cage in case people should notice and understand her longing.

Items are sold, one by one. And the man who holds up each of them so that the crowd can see them clearly is moving slowly closer to the lonely bird in its cage. People who made purchases at the start of the sale have paid and are already leaving, clutching objects to their chests. One woman has borrowed a trolley and is wheeling away an armchair.

There is no sign of Rob.

'Lot number sixty-seven!' shouts the auctioneer. His assistant lifts the cage high, for all to see. 'A musical box in the form of a songbird in a cage!'

Everyone stares at the shabby bird in its cage, raised in the air and briefly important.

'Seen better days, I'm afraid. But a nice object! What shall we say? Start me at £10!'

Zara trembles and clutches her £20 note. She had expected the bird to be worth hundreds.

No one bids. 'Five then!' says the auctioneer.

Still no bid. The auctioneer is cross. 'All right, then, let's not waste time! Start me at *one* pound!'

Everyone feels ashamed, like a class of guilty children facing a disappointed teacher.

The man in the corduroy jacket puts up his hand and calls out, 'A pound!'

An elderly lady shouts, 'Two!'

'Three!' says the corduroy man.

'Four!' says the lady.

'Five!'

The auctioneer leads the two bidders up the scale, pound by pound, and Zara watches, her heart walloping in her chest. *It's not fair*, she thinks. Neither of them wants the bird as much as *she* wants it!

When the man has reached fifteen pounds, the old lady drops out of the bidding. She shakes her head, and the auctioneer looks round at his audience.

'Going for fifteen pounds! Any more bids? Your last chance, ladies and gentlemen! Any advance on fifteen pounds?' He sweeps his eyes over his audience, like searchlights, seeking another bidder.

There is no other bidder – except Zara, who puts up her hand and says, 'Sixteen.'

That is when her life should have changed. That is the moment when she should have taken possession of the object of her desire. But that isn't what happens. And Zara understands – for the millionth time in her life – that no one has heard her. No one has seen her. She might as well be invisible.

'Sixteen pounds!' she says again. Desperately she says it, and she has her hand up, but to no effect. What came out must have been a feeble whisper, an utterance of such timidity that no one notices she has spoken. No one seems to have noticed that she is even *there*.

She is of no significance and little value. Like the bird, with its dust and rust, its chipped paint and its soundless mechanical voice.

The auctioneer cannot waste time on such a shabby object, worth only fifteen pounds. After one final searching gaze among the crowd, he raises his left hand and bangs on his desk. 'Sold to Mr Reeve!' he says. 'For fifteen pounds!'

He and Mr Reeve have known each other for years.

Zara can't bear to look at the bird in its cage. But, without intending to, she catches its unblinking eye as the man with horrible fingers (how she hates him!) picks up his new possession. The movement jerks the clockwork briefly into action, and the bird's beak opens and shuts, soundlessly telling Zara how much it wanted her to buy it. *Help!* it says, unheard.

She is embarrassed and ashamed. She needs to get out, so that no one sees that her eyes are filling with tears. As she passes the boy in the hood, he sticks his hand out. He says something meaningless that sounds like "shake down, babe!" and gives her half a bar of chocolate.

Blindly, she takes it and says thanks. Later, she wonders: *is that really what he said?* "Shake down, babe!" And had she thanked him?

'What's wrong?' says Rob when he comes back. He always knows. 'What's happened?'

She wasn't going to tell him. She wasn't going to tell anyone! But she does, and Rob – as always – tries to cheer her up.

'But I had enough money,' she says. '*And no one took any notice!*'

10

ANOTHER TIME

The morning lengthens, shadows shorten. With his stick assisting, Thomas walks firmly up the warming, winding hill amid silence and larksong. Quickly past the end of Pesthouse Lane for fear of the plague. A hilltop stone informs all travellers that there is a mile to go. It's all downhill now. The top of the church can be seen ahead, with the town around it, below him.

He hides the hazel stick in a hazel hedge to be collected later.

'I'll be back for you, stick.'

And so into Walden, through Cucking-Stool End and Golde Street, to the market square.

There are men as rich as kings and labourers as poor as beggars. There are women broad and grand like duchesses. There are cattle dealers, sheep dealers, horse dealers, sellers of hens, ferrets, rabbits, snares, cheeses, hams, cloths, yarns, threads. There are voices shouting, greeting, bargaining, complaining, scolding, laughing, and cursing.

And there are the watchful eyes of the bread-starved poor.

In the middle of the square, on a stool borrowed from the Rose and Crown, with a mug of cider beside him, sits the seven-foot Banbury giant. His hat is higher, his shoulders broader and his voice deeper than all others in the square. He is a Samson in rags. He is enthroned. He commands the market. The children of Walden and all its villages are at his feet, ensnared by little books.

'Come now!' he bellows. 'See my pedlar's pack! Pay your respects to one of the honourable companies of running stationers!'

His lungs must be as deep as the ocean.

'I have godly books, bawdy books, old street ballads, histories and penny merriments! I have books from Derby, books from London, books from York and books from Banbury. I have bestiaries and battledores. Books for sixpence and books for a penny or tuppence coloured!'

Spread at his feet are wooden boxes, tiny coffins stocked with living stories, books in bundles neatly stacked, tidily tied with string. Here are *Jack and the Giants*, *The Life of a Fly*, *Robin Hood of Sherwood Forest*, the whole story of *Robinson Crusoe* in only sixteen pages, and *Guides for Sinners to Repent*.

'Come, all ye buyers, pack your pockets with pages! Find a fistful of fictions from my chestful of cheap books!'

Which to choose?

'Have you a bawdy book, sir?'

The Banbury giant looks Thomas in the eye. 'For you?'

'No, sir. For the man who cuts the hedges.'

The giant nods and offers *The History of Jack Horner*, printed in Derby. 'You are not to read it yourself, mind. Don't open the pages! Bawdy *bites!*'

Thomas doesn't believe this nonsense. But he chooses for himself and for Mother and Father. More books are taken from bundles and stacks, and the deal is done.

Scissors! He has to buy some scissors for his mother.

There's a young woman, seated on a stool behind a long table. Thomas thinks she is very beautiful. She is the kind of woman you might see dancing by moonlight in the middle of a wood. If you're lucky. She sells wools and silks and linens, buttons and buckles and bows, needles and pins, ribbons in rolls. And sewing scissors.

'How much are these?' Thomas asks.

'Ninepence,' she says, smiling. 'For your mother?'

'Yes. Are they sharp?'

The young woman reaches over the table and takes a finger-and-thumb-full of Thomas's hair. *Snip snip!* He hears the crisp crunch of hair being sliced. 'See!' she says. 'They are neat and sharp. And they will last your mother's lifetime!'

Glowing with the pride of a journey done and bargains struck, Thomas seeks a place of silence, for reading. Abbey Lane is quiet, with only an old dame and her dog at her cottage door.

She admonishes Thomas. 'Don't go near the water, do you hear? There's danger there.'

Round the corner, by the pond, he sits against a gatepost at the edge of the town. He can see no sign of danger.

And now for reading!

*

But there is to be no peace and quiet. Girls and boys come out to play, a crowd of them. There is laughter and shouting. Stones are thrown; ducks are driven cackling away; and the old woman in the lane waves her stick and goes inside.

There will be no more peace. They too have been buying their Banbury books.

There is a quarrel. A girl called Bell – with bare, dusty feet and a long, raggedy dress – says that her great-grandma has a *Dick Whittington* just like this one but better.

Better than this one? No one believes her. *Liar! Liar!*

Bell stretches her upper half at them like an angry goose and tells them what she thinks of them. 'I don't *care*!' she says and starts to cry, caring bitterly. 'I'm *not* a liar!' she says.

Children share reading. In their books they find Banbury Cross, Banbury cakes and Banbury bridge. Most rhymes lead to Banbury.

Master John the Quaker hobbles by the pond with a quick and watchful eye on the boys and girls. Once he taught them their spellings, but now he waves his walking stick and mutters to himself. His business is piety and primers. He wants nothing to do with Banbury books.

'Good afternoon, Master John.'

He says not a word and turns away. They have disappointed him. They are full of guilt and giggling.

A printer's apprentice is sitting on a stile, glowering like a crow. He pulls his shabby black coat around his shoulders, climbs down from the stile and slouches towards them. His upper body stoops and swings from side to side with every step.

Some of the children draw back. 'Don't go near him,' a girl whispers to Thomas. 'He's a printer's devil!'

The printer's devil glares at them with dark, hooded eyes.

A little girl is crying at the edge of the pond.

'What's the matter with you, Kitty?'

'My ma beat me.'

'What for?'

'I only had tuppence and I went and wasted it.'

'What on?'

'I bought a Banbury book and it's a dud.'

'A dud?'

'It's not a proper book.'

They all crowd round and look. Kitty's book is *The Interesting Story of the Children in the Wood.*

'It's better than ours,' big Bell says to little Kitty. 'Your pictures are coloured.' It's true, and Kitty brightens up a little. The robbers in her book have yellow breeches and blue cloaks, and there are bright drops of red blood. None of the other books have drops of red blood. Or any colour at all. Just black, on white paper.

Kitty stands by as all the children look. They have

never seen a book with colours in. It is a wondrous thing!

But it's not a book at all, just a single sheet of paper. How can you call that a *book*? And the printed pages are in the wrong order, eight on one side and eight on the other. Half of them are upside down! The children turn to the printer's apprentice, hoping he will use his devil knowledge and put the matter to rights.

That's what he does. 'The sheet must be folded properly,' he tells them. 'And cut and stitched. Then it will be a book.'

Can a single sheet of paper be turned into a book, with proper pages? Is this some kind of printer's magic?

'This is what you do,' the devil apprentice says. He folds the paper once, twice and a third time, tight and neat. Then it is almost a book, with the title on the front where it should be. But it's not quite a book because you can't open the pages. 'The edges have to be trimmed,' he says.

Mother's new sewing scissors are offered and the children crowd round. He shows Kitty (no longer crying) what must be done. With black and inky fingers, he trims three of the edges as neatly and narrowly as if they were a baby's fingernails. 'The top edge must be cut, and the bottom too,' he says. 'Then the right-hand edge. But not the left. Leave that folded.'

Kitty is wide-eyed and half in love with the magical apprentice. For the rest of her life, she will remember him. Her flat and meaningless paper has been magically changed into a tiny book like all the others but better than the others because it has coloured pictures. Out of confusion, a story has appeared. The rhymes are in their proper places; all the pages are the same way up; and now they are in the correct order.

It is amazing! The children in the wood are captured and caught for the fate that awaits them.

'I'll hold it together with a pin,' says the printer's apprentice. 'When you get home, ask your mam to stitch the pages together along the fold. One big stitch will be enough, and then you can take out the pin.'

Kitty's face is all thanks. But someone whispers to Thomas: 'Where did he get that pin from? I *told* you he was a devil!' The devil apprentice returns Mother's scissors and goes back to his stile where he sits, hunched and glaring, clutching his coat around his shoulders like a black crow.

Suddenly the pond is left in silence. The children have gone back to the market and the Banbury man. Everyone who has some pennies left wants to buy a copy of *The Children in the Wood* in bright colours. So that they can fold it and make it into a proper book. And look happily at the bright drops of blood pouring out.

Thoughts of scissors bring to mind thoughts of Mother. And Mother brings to mind Father. *I have a long way to go*, Thomas thinks.

Why should Mother and Father want him to go so far away for a whole long summer's day?

11

THIS TIME

Zara's day has been bruised and won't get better. It's because of what happened at the auction.

Rob thinks of a plan to distract her. He borrows his dad's wellington boots and his mum's, and they wade into the bright stream to search for more coloured stones.

They find three more, each with a single flat, coloured surface. Two are eggshell blue, one a deep rose-pink.

This is pleasant, but Zara's bruise remains. She knows the next day will probably be better, and Thursday will be great because Dad will be coming home. But today is spoiled.

But it's Rob's day as well as Zara's. 'You're ruining it,' he says. He is stern with her.

'Can we go to Howe's Wood?' she asks him.

Rob knows that the meaning of her words is: *I'm sorry. I'll try harder. Going to Howe's Wood will help to cheer me up.*

She is contrite.

'Good idea!' he says.

He goes into the house and comes back with a packet of biscuits, two bags of crisps and a bottle of drink. He tells his mum where they're going.

They set off – over the hills and far away to one of Zara's favourite places in the world. She is trying hard to drive away her thoughts about the auction.

The bruise is fading. Just a bit. And she's feeling happier.

They meet a travelling monster, an obstruction on wheels. It is a farm vehicle as big as a house, taking up most of the road. Its tyres are as high as a garage door and fat like an elephant's body. The driver is remote and lofty. *When he went past my house*, Zara thinks, *he could have looked right into my bedroom. He's so high he would have looked* down *into my bedroom!*

She has a brief picture in her head of her blue pyjamas thrown carelessly on the bed. ('Have you tidied your bedroom?' Mum asked.) And if he'd looked carefully, he might have seen yesterday's bra and knickers that she'd forgotten to put with the dirty linen.

But he probably hadn't looked. He is intent and severe, seeing nothing but the road in front. His ears are padded for protection, or perhaps he is listening to music. Behind his vehicle, two massive harrow bars are raised to the sky, pointed. The machine has its hands together and is saying its prayers.

Despite its great weight, the tractor bounces with a massive and jaunty carelessness. Zara and Rob press into the grassy bank until it has passed. Behind it there is a bad-tempered convoy, unable to overtake. Two cars, a small lorry and a red post office van.

Zara and Rob leave the road and set off along a farm track. But there's a problem: a notice at the edge of the wood says "STRICTLY PRIVATE NO ENTRY". But they both know that the path goes right through the wood, and there's no notice at the other end. 'We might have come in from the other direction, and then we wouldn't know we aren't allowed,' Rob says reasonably.

Equally reasonably, Zara points out: 'But we didn't. We're coming from *this* direction. And we *have* seen the notice!'

Every time they come here, they have a lawyer's discussion about the rights and wrongs of this. It's an old game they started when they were nine or ten. They always conclude that it's legal to walk one way through the wood but illegal to walk the other. 'So if we see the owner, we just have to turn round and walk the other way,' Rob says. 'Then we won't be breaking the law.'

But they both know the owner is old Mr Waller, who is so frail that he can hardly walk to the end of his garden, let alone into the middle of his wood.

Zara's spirits lift. The bruise of the day fades a little more.

The way through the wood is a wide, green lane, sunlit and open to the sky and covered with fresh spring grass peppered and salted with buttercups and cow parsley. On each side, the trees crowd thickly together, still and concentrating.

Zara no longer believes in fairies and elves, but she hasn't abandoned them entirely. And she still asks herself: *Who made this green road? And what is it for?*

And (the best part of the mystery) *why is there a milestone in the middle of a wood?* Why would anyone place a milestone there, where no travellers travel?

The wood is a green and shadowy city, and its citizens are in hiding. Millions of them. Thousands of tiny eyes, watching. Thousands of ears, pricked and attentive. Thousands of tiny snouts, anxiously quivering. Zara feels goose pimples on the back of her neck, loving it. Then, in the quietness, they hear the song of a wren close by, cold and sharp, like tiny beads of ice on a thread of snow. Zara catches the bird's eye briefly as it flickers like a tiny shadow from one branch to another.

There is a crossroad. Another silent, grassy highway crosses the first one.

There ought to be a great bustle here at the crossroad. Carriages and carts coming and going, travellers with bags and baskets, voices talking, shouting, laughing. But there is only the sunlit silence and a white hawthorn snowing its petals onto the grass and the buttercups.

And there is the milestone, covered tightly with moss like miniature grass, as neat and trimmed as if it were tended by tiny elf-gardeners climbing little ladders.

But there's someone else. Coming towards them from the other direction, the legal direction.

A man, with a gun tucked under his arm.

Danger?

But it's not a gun. Zara can see that it's a walking stick,

and he is carrying something large on a strap over his shoulder. Some kind of camera.

A stranger in the wood! 'Don't leave the path,' Rob's mum always says. But what if bad people walk on the path too? And you meet them there?

Common sense, however, must sometimes rule. She sees that this stranger could not give chase. The closer he comes, the clearer it is that he is limping.

'Hello!' he says cheerfully. He lowers himself onto the milestone. It's a long way down because he's a tall man with long legs. Sighing with relief, he lays down his stick and camera.

Zara and Rob stand, at a safe distance. 'Hello,' Rob says.

'What are you doing here?' the man says. 'Two children in an empty forest! Are you taking food to your sick grandmother? Shouldn't one of you be wearing a red hood?'

There is no sick grandmother; she doesn't exist. But that does not stop Zara from feeling indignant. This man is a stranger and has no right to ask questions.

But Rob is untroubled. 'We're just walking. We know the owner.'

'Mr Waller! I know him too. Nice old chap.'

'What are you doing?' Rob asks.

He thinks for a moment, perhaps wondering if he can trust them. 'I'm a story seller,' he says. 'I'm looking for a story.'

That's just silly, Zara thinks. But the stranger explains a little. 'I sell stories,' he says. 'But first I have to find them.'

'Who do you sell them to?'

'Television people, mostly. Websites too. Magazines and newspapers.'

'Have you been on the telly?' Rob asks.

'No. I'm not a presenter. But you might have heard my voice-over. And seen my stories.'

What Zara sees at that moment is a weasel rippling across the silent highway and disappearing into the trees with its tail joyously twitching like a squirrel's. She has a brief mind picture of shadowy animal lives (no more than a flashing image, like the weasel's tail).

'I had a story last week, on the local news programme. You might have seen it. It's on YouTube too. About a pair of peregrine falcons nesting in Cambridge. On the roof of the university library.'

I saw that, Zara remembers. She is impressed. So he *is* a real-life story seller! In her wood!

'What story are you looking for here?' Rob says.

'Orchids,' the stranger says. 'I've been told…'

'We can show you where they are,' Rob says. 'But they're only the common ones. The spotted ones.' He looks at Zara for confirmation.

It was Zara who found the orchids. She is their expert on wild flowers.

'I suspected as much,' the stranger says sadly. 'Not much of a story there then. Pity really! People are being told all the time that they should get back in touch with wildlife. Now, if there'd been *bee* orchids…'

Stalemate. No one can think of anything to say.

'What will you do for a story then?' That is Zara speaking, surprising herself (and Rob).

The stranger shows no surprise because he doesn't know that Zara normally keeps her tongue tied. He slowly straightens his long, bad leg. 'I might be sitting on one,' he says. 'Milestones are for busy roads and highways full of traffic. Why is there one in the middle of an empty wood?'

It's not *empty*, Zara thinks.

The stranger rises to his feet, unsteadily, and turns to study the milestone. 'Pity about the moss. I can't make out what it says.'

But Rob and Zara know what is carved on the milestone. 'It says "Walden III m. London XL m". And there are two arrows, one pointing in each direction,' Rob adds.

'Who put it here?' the stranger wonders.

The elves, Zara thinks. But she knows she can't say that. It's just something she liked to pretend when she was little.

'We could dig down beside it,' the story seller says thoughtfully.

'Why?'

'There might be a mason's mark carved on it. Or a date.'

He sees that Zara and Rob disapprove of this suggestion. 'You always have to dig,' he says. 'People look for history in churches and castles. And in libraries, of course. But the best history is always *in the ground*. Under your feet. You have to dig to find it.'

He is making this into a story, Zara thinks. Rob says, 'We found this in a stream.' He digs into his trouser pocket and holds out his hand, with the coloured, flat stones embedded in a small lump of cement.

The stranger studies the stones. 'They're not stones,' he says thoughtfully. 'They're called *tesserae*. Better than orchids.'

Zara takes hold of Rob's hand and draws back a little. There is just the tiniest hint of something strange, like a sudden shadow chilling the warmth of the sun. Perhaps all story sellers have a flicker of danger about them. A touch of darkness.

But it passes as quickly as it came. 'You should *dig*,' the stranger says. 'Stop looking in the river. You should dig nearby! In the earth.'

Dig?

An abrupt change of mood. 'Now!' he says. 'I'm going to take some pictures of this milestone and these green roads which no one ever uses. Perhaps I can make a story out of it. Who knows?'

He lays down his stick and picks up his camera.

'And,' he adds, 'if you find any more of these stones, send me an email. They could be Roman.'

He hands Zara a card – rovingstory@btinternet.com – along with a phone number, a website and a postal address in Norwich. She puts it in the pocket of her jeans.

Roman? Does he mean it? Is he telling the truth?

Rob is not to be tricked. 'But if we do find anything, it will be *our* story, not yours.'

'A story belongs to the teller,' the stranger says.

Stories belong to everyone, Zara thinks. But, as usual, she says nothing.

12

THE FIRST TIME

There was bread for breakfast. Old, grey bread. Juliana broke it into two hunks and gave me the bigger part.

The low winter sun rose in the bitter dawn. It melted the hoar frost and shone on our faces. But the earth was still hard and frozen. I heard a cock crowing. There were hens in the ruins. The cock and hens were unafraid of Roman ghosts. Juliana walked among the tumbled walls and searched from place to place.

She shared her breakfast with me. Six eggs in an iron pan and more bread.

'How old are you?' I asked Juliana.

'Twelve summers and thirteen winters,' she said.

She was thin and her black hair was like a horse's mane. Her small hands were rough and red, her nails round and neatly bitten.

'Who made this place?' I asked her.

'My grandfather,' she said.

But this was a puzzle to me.

I remembered the flame bird, staring with no eye.

Another puzzle.

Before I left, I showed her Guthlac's leather bag. I spilled out the gifts onto a Roman stone. The gold shone in the pale morning sun. It was a small hoard, a story-teller's gold gifts. I told her they were given by great men for his stories. He was a song singer for kings.

'Battle heroes have bigger gift hoards than story-tellers,' I told her.

Juliana asked me: 'Did the people of the village give you gifts for Guthlac's stories?'

'Yes, but not gold. Two chickens' legs and some leeks. And hard cheese.'

She nodded. That was as it should be.

Then I told her to take a gift from Guthlac's hoard. 'You saved my life,' I said.

She would not choose. I gave her a bracelet of beads, amber, bone and coloured glass, threaded on silver wire. I pushed aside her sleeve and slipped the bracelet over her narrow wrist.

'I will hide it,' she said. 'From robbers and murderers. I will make a hiding place here, close by the bird.'

*

We said farewell, Juliana the lifesaver and Sæwara the gift-giver. She wore the bracelet, proudly smiling, holding out her wrist. When I looked back, she had gone.

Was she a spirit? Was Juliana a Roman ghost haunting the ghost house? Or was she a girl-hero?

I saw five men on a hillside, against the sky, walking, small on the land edge. One stopped and saw me, the keen one.

They were far away, but they turned and followed me.

I hurried over the melting hoar frost in the cold winter sun, sometimes walking, sometimes running, always homewards.

Once I stopped and turned. When we were young, Eadweard taught me unclean words of scorn. We whispered them to each other and laughed. Remembering, I hooped my hands around my mouth and yelled at the five followers, 'May your mouths be full of turds!' My voice was clear in the cold sky. One of the men lifted his fist, clenched. 'May your beards be full of shit! May your balls freeze and fall off!'

I knew my fate, the lust in their groins, if they saw I was a woman. But I was not frightened of the Guthlac-killers. I was fast.

But in my heart, I wept for Guthlac. He was in my thoughts, lying in his frozen lifeblood. I asked the gods' forgiveness for not burying him in the stone-hard earth.

As I hastened homewards to the kinsfolk of my village, I made a riddle for Guthlac. One step for each word. One breath for each thought.

story storer
lyre lover
way walker

country crosser
dragon dreamer
mead master
memory maker
dream drawer
tale teller
stream stepper
hill strider
word weaver.

I stopped in my running and my riddle-making, and I looked back. The five followers were still in sight. They were closer now. The leader held a long knife in his right hand.

Soon, clouds hid the face of the sun and the bird road was grey. Snow fell, and the bitter wind chilled my feet and hands.

There was a hoodie crow in a tree. Its body was grey, its head and beak were glossy black. It eyed me balefully as I passed. There are hoodies in our spells and stories, always watchful. We are wary of hoodies. It lifted itself into the air and flew heavily away, knocking snow from the branches. *Craaw!* It said to me as it flew over, heavy and slow and straight, alone in the grey falling sky.

Was the hoodie a messenger from the lower world? Had it spoken? What use is a message if it cannot be understood?

Guthlac was like a hoodie crow, dark and stooping. Was this Guthlac's spirit, speaking to me?

I honoured Guthlac in my heart, the brave traveller.

'All things fail, all things are laid low,' he said. 'Fate brings death and sorrow, greatness is brought down. No man or woman can hold back fate.'

He spoke like that. It was his way. I knew the thoughts of his heart, and I honoured him. But my own heart was young and filled with hope. I hurried on towards my homecoming.

When I looked back, I could not see the murderers through the thick snowfall. I did not know where they were.

13

ANOTHER TIME

The streets of the town are rivers of heat in the summer evening. Time to go home now – over the hills and far away. It has been a long, long day. When Thomas reaches the top of the first hill, he feels weariness gathering in legs and feet.

At the end of Pesthouse Lane, the walking stick waits in the hedgerow for its owner.

Home now, stick!

For the next mile, the two of them make good three-legged progress over the hill and down towards the cottages at Rose Farm. There is cheerfulness in the birdsong of evening and comfort in the quiet sounds of cattle tearing the grass on the other side of tall hedges. So it's a shock to walk firmly round the bend at the bottom of the hill and find Old Lopsy lying in wait, beside the big pond. He is crouching in his old pine chair, staring at his boots, just as he has sat (so they say) for nigh on twenty years.

His head snaps round. His terrible old whiskers are a-dribble as he stares at the startled child.

'Show me! You!'

The pond is still and black in the evening light. But it is no good looking up the garden path for the young woman with a rolling pin in her hand. She is nowhere to be seen. There can be no rescue this time. A tired young boy with a stick must stand against a bony old man with violence in his heart.

'*Show me!* Show me, or I'll twist your skinny little neck!'

What does he want? One of the geese laughs from the far side of the pond. *Honk, honk, honk, honk!* This sets off the others, and they all laugh loudly.

'You're a smelly French spy!'

'I'm not! I'm not a French spy!' Thomas speaks firmly.

'What's in that pouch?'

'Books. I'm not smelly, either.'

'What sort of books?'

'Storybooks. Little ones.'

'*French* storybooks!'

'No. Banbury books. I bought them from the Banbury man at the market.'

Old Lopsy stares.

'From the Banbury man?' he says. His lips flick spit and his quivery old mouth looks like a damp doorway to somewhere unknown.

Thomas nods.

'Show me!'

So Thomas opens the bag and takes out the penny books. Old Lopsy's thick devil's fingernails hold in their horniness the Fairy, Bluebeard, tiny Tom Thumb and the rest. He will tear them all to bits, certainly. Or spit on them in his rage, or throw them into the pond, or steal them away and keep them for himself.

But a change has come over Old Lopsy. He has thrown off his wolf's clothing and is as meek as a lamb. He whispers to Thomas with eagerness in his voice. 'Is he still coming then? Same as ever?'

'Yes.'

'How tall is he now?'

'Tall as a house. Nearly.'

'He always was! He always was! To think that he's still coming! From Banbury, you say?'

'Yes, sir.'

'He's been coming ever since Roman times! Did you know that?'

'No, sir.'

'I wish I could go to market again.'

Old Lopsy's head is on one side, and his eyes are full of longing.

'Will you read to me, boy?'

'I'm tired, sir. And it's getting dark.'

'Just one.' The old man wheedles and pleads and settles back in his chair full of attention and eagerness.

'Which one shall I read?'

'*Guy of Warwick*. Ah, he's a real hero!'

While the weary traveller reads *Guy of Warwick*,

Old Lopsy sits as quiet as a bedtime four-year-old in the lengthening shadows. When the reading is done, the old, mad head nods in appreciation.

He hands back the other books, and his toothless old mouth forms a quivering crescent-moon smile. He is so happy that he is crying! Why can that be? Why does Old Lopsy rise, shaking and knobbly-gripping the arms of his chair? Is it because Guy of Warwick has come back? Just as he did in the reign of King George I?

'They were all there,' he says, 'when I was a boy. Bevis of Southampton and Richard Whittington and Robin Hood. And to think that they're still coming to Walden market! Old Guy hasn't changed a bit after all these years!'

'I must go now,' Thomas says.

'Ah, so you must!' Old Lopsy says kindly, still sniffling shamelessly. 'There are all kinds of dangers on the road after dark, y'know.'

'Goodbye.'

'When we used to play on Walden Common...' Old Lopsy says sadly. 'Ah, I was a scrap of a boy in them days, no bigger'n you.'

Thomas – driven off in the morning with young, round potatoes and rewarded in the evening with an old man's thanks – is full of tired puzzlement as the next hill is climbed. Can Guy of Warwick and Robin Hood do so much? Have they such power? Can they thread Old Lopsy's childhood with Thomas's, lacing everyone together in patterns as old as the Romans?

In the dusk, hedgerows and hawthorns, campion

and cow parsley, leaves and lanes, are changed – changed and charged by chapbooks, filled with fictions, peopled with possibilities. And all for a penny! The old wooden signpost that says "To Wimbish" might just as easily point to Sherwood Forest or Banbury Cross or China.

*

The hedge cutter is nowhere to be seen. His hedge-weaving is done for the day, and he has gone home to his bawdy-loving daughter. Thomas pushes *Jack Horner* into the crack in the gatepost. He's glad to keep a promise without being delayed by more talking.

In the flaky yellow lichen on the gate, some strange spellings have been scratched. "Tak theſe ſtix fur the bbs".

What can this mean? Is it bawdy language? In the grass are two neatly trimmed hazel sticks, smaller than the one cut in the morning. Walking sticks for dwarfs.

They are further payment, perhaps, for *Jack Horner*. But what does "bbs" mean? How much longer will it take him to reach home? And what use are two short sticks?

*

With twelve penny chapbooks and a pair of scissors in his bag, two short sticks in one hand and a long stick in the other, Thomas approaches the house of Uncle William. Thoughts of Aunt Meg's saffron cake give encouragement for aching legs and tired feet.

And afterwards, Uncle William will walk with him the rest of the way home.

But Uncle William is not in his garden, and Aunt Meg is not in her kitchen.

He lifts the latch, steps cautiously over the threshold and stands listening to the house's silence, motionless, reflecting. The table, chairs, dresser and stove, the jugs, mugs, platters and pans, the knives, skewers, ladles and spoons all look knowingly at each other, like mean children excluding a friend from a secret. The only sound is the solemn ticking of the wall clock which hangs in its long, glass-fronted box. It's known as grandmother's clock, and it's treated with respect.

Tick tock, nobody here, says the clock.

Hunger has already joined tiredness, and now there are loneliness and fear too. Aunt Meg is always in the kitchen, and Uncle William is always in the garden. It's a law of the universe that they should be there. So what is a boy to make of it when they're not?

Tiredness and hunger – and the strange emptiness of the house – have stolen away his boy's courage. He has become about six years old again. Grandmother's clock has brought grandmother to mind, and now mind recalls what memory has carefully shut out: the image of the loved old lady dying. Did someone give *her* storybooks when she was a girl? Did she play with Old Lopsy on Walden Common when they were children?

And where is she now? In heaven? In that long box in the chalky graveyard? Or does she somehow live inside her clock, to send her grandson away, tired and scared.

Is *anything* safe?

It's almost dark, Thomas thinks, keeping an anxious eye on the twilight bats swooping and sweeping over the darkening lane.

14

THIS TIME

In the time of one of Rob's great-great-great ancestors, a branch was cut from an apple tree. A generation later, a round hole rotted itself into existence where the cut had been made. Inside, the wood decayed into powder, and after another twenty years, the hole became a hollow entrance.

Perfect for nesting great tits.

In the bright blue morning, a pair of them are busy. Their movements flutter soundlessly as they bring food and fly away for more. They know that people are nearby, but they're untroubled by them. Their work is urgent.

Below them, by the stream, Zara and Rob have been digging all morning. 'Dig!' the story seller said. 'If you want to find the oldest history, you have to *dig*!'

Lying on the grass nearby are their finds, carefully washed in the stream. Each is a small piece of history.

A yellow plastic yo-yo, without its string. ('I remember that!' Rob's dad says joyfully. 'That was mine!')

Lots of broken china, mostly blue and white. ('Perhaps people quarrelled a lot in those days and threw cups and saucers at each other,' Rob suggests.)

Two old red bricks, just like the bricks of the farmhouse.

An old knife, its bone handle more or less intact but the blade browned and blistered hard with rust.

A small china doll, glazed and white. (Rob's mum knows what that is. 'My granny had some of them – she used to put them into Christmas puddings.')

Some shards of pottery. (Broken flowerpots, they tell each other.)

This is all history, Zara thinks, *but it's not historical enough.*

After lunch it begins to rain, but the four labourers continue – two fluttering silently in and out of the tree, nurturing the future, and two on the ground, digging up the past.

'When you've finished,' Rob's dad says severely, 'all those holes will have to be filled in!'

They dig on, doggedly, carefully, feeling with mud-encrusted fingers through each spadeful of earth before it's piled on one side.

'You're soaked!' Rob's mum says.

Rob finds a sinister dark-blue bottle. 'Poison,' he says. In letters of raised glass on the side are the words "NOT TO BE TAKEN". Zara washes the bottle in the stream and puts it with their other discoveries. Then – too late

– she wonders if she has poisoned all the fish, but the tiny minnows and sticklebacks that she can see modestly darting in the water seem to be untroubled. And alive.

'You can have all these things for your museum,' Rob says.

'I don't want the bricks,' says Zara.

'*Stop now!*' Rob's mum says firmly. This time she means it. 'It's nearly time for Zara to go home, and you're both absolutely *soaked!*'

She tells them to go inside, have a bath and dry their clothes. But as Zara straightens up, her eye catches something shining in the earth at her feet.

Glass.

But not a bottle. It's half of a perfect circle, and when they lift it clear, it leaves an exact print of itself in the damp earth. They wash it and inspect it as it lies in the pale palm of Zara's hand.

Rob's mum forgets about having a bath and drying their clothes. 'Half of a bangle,' she whispers.

It's not like any glass they have seen. It has been roughened a little by having been buried in the earth. But – most strangely and most beautifully – it is rainbowy all through. A tiny, solid rainbow.

Rob's mum takes Zara's hand and holds the bangle against her wrist, where it would be perfect if they had all of it. The rest of Zara's body has a fit of the shivers.

More digging, scrabbling rather, for they are tired and wet and over-eager.

But they can't find the other half of the bangle. 'Never mind,' Rob's mum says. 'I think this might be *very* old.'

How old, they want to know.

'I think it might be Roman.'

Roman! Could this be a story for the story seller? But Rob shakes his head. 'It's only half a story,' he says.

As she peels off her wet clothes in Rob's bathroom, Zara wonders if that is all history can ever be. Half-stories. She shivers, goes goose pimply all over and steps into the warm bath.

*

On Thursday morning there is more digging. With their backs bent, they are unaware that five fledgling great tits are queuing up inside their nest to launch themselves into life. The first one peeps briefly out into the future, plops soundlessly out and miraculously flies away. Immediately, the next one is at the entrance, then the third and fourth. The last one takes longer to look round before fluttering anxiously to a nearby branch of the tree.

This new great tit generation has taken no more than three minutes to leave home for good. Into the dangerous world they leap!

Zara spots a muddy object in the side of their hole. She scrapes it clean with her spade. It is a heavy square brick, or tile. About thirty centimetres across and three centimetres thick and a dark reddish-brown. After they have poured water over it, they can see that a rough circular pattern has been drawn on it, with the point of a knife or a builder's trowel.

In one corner there is a thumbprint, baked hard into the clay. They try their thumbs against it, but this thumb was broad. A big grown-up working thumb.

'A historical thumb,' Zara says. She says an imaginary hello to the long-ago potter with big thumbs.

The clay brick is embedded in the hard, wet earth. Rob pushes the spade under one edge and levers it up so that it stands vertical. Under it, bright but grimy in the sunlight, is a small circlet of coloured beads, waiting to be found. It seems to speak to them, saying, *at last!*

This one is not half a bangle. It is the complete object, perfect. '*Oh!*' Zara whispers in rapture.

She runs her fingertips over the beads: amber and coloured glass, blue, red and green. And when she moves them, she finds they are strung on some kind of black wire.

'They might have belonged to Cleopatra,' Rob speculates. But Zara – as she holds the beads in the palm of her hand, studying them, loving them – thinks not.

She takes the bracelet to the stream and rinses away the dirt. The coloured glass winks in the sunshine.

'Put it on,' Rob says. 'It's meant for a girl.'

But Zara shakes her head. She has no right.

But there is a new impetus now, a confidence driving them on. You wouldn't find a Roman brick (perhaps) and one-and-a-half Roman bracelets (perhaps) in the middle of nowhere! This must be *somewhere*, they feel sure. Somewhere historical.

Their next find is too big to be shifted. A great stone, roughly rectangular. And others next to it, stretching beyond in a line. 'We need a soft brush,' Rob says.

In her excitement, Zara races indoors and forgets to be tongue-tied long enough to ask Rob's mum for a brush. She is given two.

The earth is soft and fine. Carefully, they brush the big stones clean and clear. But they are too heavy to be moved, fixed and solid in the ground. 'We should dig down beside them,' Rob says.

More digging, more sweeping.

They are gripped, both of them, tense with the excitement of discovery. As they brush away the soil, something new appears: a flat surface made of coloured stones pressed into a pattern. Grey and white they are, and roughly square, and they form an interlocking design of lines and right angles.

Carefully, they widen their digging, and more is uncovered. They find different stones fixed there, blue, lemon and rose-pink.

Rob can make no sense of it. 'It's a tail!' Zara says. 'They're feathers! It's a picture of a bird's tail. Made of small, coloured stones!'

Unnoticed, Rob's mum has come up behind them and is staring. 'Oh, my God!' she says softly. '*Now* what?'

She has always longed to find a rare antique.

15

THE FIRST TIME

Hunger gnawed my belly. The snowfall was bitter. My eyes were wet with grief for Guthlac, and the tears froze on my face.

A crow had croaked over me.

The falling flakes grew thin. The clouds parted, and a strip of sky turned pale. The snow stopped falling. There were dark clouds all around. The sun was low and as cold and white as the moon.

Behind me I heard a shout. The five killers were closer, running hard. I was on a trackway, crossing a wide and windswept hilltop.

I must be-thin myself to nothing. I was good at hiding. I could climb trees, bury myself in the winter growth of a ditch or crouch unseen in shadows. But on the hillside, there were no trees, no ditches and no shadows. They could see me, like a small tree, bare and black against the bright snow.

Ahead, the road ran down and deep, between high fields. Out of the wind, out of the killers' sight.

I remembered Guthlac, breathing hard and grumbling as we climbed up the hill, on our way to the hall of Rædwald.

Two of the killers were fast and out in front, the leader with his knife drawn and wearing Guthlac's cloak and another carrying a wooden club. The other three followed behind.

Guthlac's harp chest was heavy on my back. It hindered me in my running.

The trackway was covered with new snow, a finger's depth. How could I find a place for hiding without leaving footmarks?

I did not lose hope. I sped over the hillside and down to the deep trackway, churning the snow. The road turned left, a sharp corner. A path came down from a field. Cows had come this way. Cows' hooves and a cowherd's feet had trodden and mushed the snow.

The cowherd's footmarks were small. A child caring for cows. There was fresh dung, steaming and new.

My footmarks were lost in the crumpled mess and mud-snow. Round the corner, I would be out of the killers' sight. They had theft and murder in their hearts. There would be rape too when they found out. Probably a killing.

The trackway turned again, this time to the right. There was a ford where a stream crossed the road. It was black and frozen, as hard as Roman stone.

Round the corner was a water place. A mere, stretching away to distant reeds, stiff and grey and winter-pale. There were five geese at the far side, white in the fading light, watching. A heron stood, like a small, leafless tree.

The pond was frozen thick and black. There was no fallen snow on the ice. The soft, cold wind blew the snow dust into swirls and curls. Every fleck of snow was driven, sliding across the smooth and shining ice.

On the windswept ice there would be no footmarks.

The leader of the killers was a shouter. I heard his voice, clear and close in the frosty stillness. They had turned the first corner, but I was round the next.

Still out of their sight.

I jumped across stiff, frozen grass, from the trackway onto the ice, leaving no marks. I stayed close to the edge of the pond. Eadweard and I knew that ice is thin in the middle of water. I skated and skidded round the frozen pond edge until I reached the farther side.

I was fast, and my feet left no marks. There was only snow-dust drifted and blown by the wind.

I pushed deep into the reeds, dry and stiff and yellow-grey. I crouched and made myself small, watching the road. Stiff, cold stalks penned me in. They were close to my face, in front of my eyes. They were in my mind, freezing and upright, whispering in the winter wind. The thicket of reeds sheltered me and hid me from the killers.

I was not a woman in danger. I was a small brown bird, a reed-dweller, watching for danger with a bright, searching eye.

My body shivered and shrank under my cloak. Snow settled on my black hood and only my eyes could be seen. My feet hurt with the cold, and my hands ached. My skin shivered and my belly was empty. But my heart was glad, for I was craftier than my enemies.

At the second corner, the two fastest runners stopped, clutching their sides. The three caught up with the two and stood with them. I could see their bodies heaving as they breathed. They looked at the ground by their feet, seeking footmarks. But the trampled snow was cattle-churned.

The shouter was the cunning one. He stood tall and gazed around. He stared first at the hillside to their right, then along the snowy trackway that stretched up the next hill, and afterwards across the frozen pond on their left.

On the hillside there were no marks. Just tall grasses pricking the snow cover. On the road there were all kinds of footmarks. Too many. On the pond there was nothing to see but ice.

And on the far side a stand of rushes. And in the rushes, a young woman hiding. Unseen and still. Like a small bird.

I was inside his head. I knew his thoughts. He was puzzled and angry.

The heron lifted herself into air. Her wings clattered in the icy stillness. She rose clumsily into the grey sky and flew slowly over the heads of the killers. They watched in anger.

I sent out my thoughts, and I became the heron. I looked down on the five killers below me with a cold eye.

I flew on, heavily, eastwards into the bitter wind. The five geese laughed loudly from the far side of the ice.

'An empty belly makes powerful dreams,' Guthlac used to say.

The leader put away his knife. They had lost their prey. I knew his mind. But he was wrong. I could send out my thoughts, but I was not a heron spirit. I did not have wings.

He pointed ahead, along the road. They set off again, slowly now, leaving me unseen inside my cold house of standing reeds, with their grey, drooping flags.

'No man can escape his fate,' Guthlac used to say. But I say that a quick and clever-witted woman can escape her enemies.

I waited. The clouds had closed above my head. They were dark and heavy with snow. Flakes began to fall again, slow and thick, with no wind. The five geese stretched their necks, raised their heads and honked their evening call. First one, then the other four. They were loud shouters.

And a small bird moved in the rushes where I crouched, sharing my shelter.

The snow fell, deep and still and soundless.

I could not stay all night. I stood and stretched. I rubbed my freezing hands and thumped my feet. Then I crossed the ice and set off along the trackway, following the killers.

I stamped and stumbled through the deepening snowfall, keeping a watchful eye on the road ahead.

I yearned for my homestead, for warmth, and food,

and drink, and friends. And for Eadweard, the warmth of his hold.

The darkness closed in. There were no stars; there was no moon, only the pale shine of the fallen snow, growing deeper.

16

THIS TIME

Professor Molly Barnes, driving her sky-blue Skoda carefully towards Chipping Walden, wonders what she will find on arrival. *A Roman mosaic?* That's what they said on the phone. It would be pleasant to end her career on a high note. But then she thinks – there's no point in talking about *ending her career*. She doesn't want to stop work, and in any case, people won't allow it. *I'm in my eighties, for heaven's sake!* But they keep inviting her to new sites, each with its own discoveries to be made.

She's not expected to organise anything these days, just to bear witness. 'Come and have a look at what we've found,' they say. And she can't resist the call.

There's cow parsley on every roadside as she drives through East Anglia. Green and white and frothy, filling the banks and verges. People call it Queen Anne's lace.

Queen Anne, Queen Anne, she sat in the sun,
Making of lace till the day was done.
She made it green, she made it white,
She made it of flowers and sunshine and light.
…Queen Anne's lace, Queen Anne's lace,
You find it growing all over the place!

Was it, she thinks, growing all over the place when the Anglo-Saxons arrived, edging the green, rutted lanes? Were their hearts lifted in joy at the sight of it faithfully returning, every May?

But that's what you can never know, she thinks. *Heart-liftings* get left out of history – the green and the white and the sunshine and especially the liftings of the heart. Left out of the archaeology too, most of the time, she thinks sadly.

Where did that rhyme come from? she wonders. From somewhere not quite lost, where Little Miss Muffet still lives, along with Jack and Jill and Old Mother Hubbard and the others? Were they already here, more than a thousand years ago? Or did the Anglo-Saxons bring them?

Or are they perhaps the diminished skeletal relics of a huge, lost mythology?

I ought to know, she thinks. *I'm an expert on the past*. She's just finished filming a documentary series for BBC2, in which she is both scriptwriter and presenter, chosen – according to the television trailer – because she has devoted her long life to archaeology. 'No one in the country knows more about our archaeology than Professor Barnes.'

But she's come to understand that the knowledge is

VICTOR WATSON

itself problematic. You uncover an object, and you clean it, question it, photograph it, subject it to tests, carbon-date it, write an academic paper about it. And after all of that, you might have learned a minute grain of something that might be called "knowledge". Yet it's always elusive, ambiguous, vanishing as you study it, turning itself into new questions. And even if, for once, you discover a single secure fact, it will be surrounded by shifting contexts, only half-understood, throwing mysteries and doubts on what you thought were certainties.

So why do I keep on doing it? She knows the answer of course. It's the joy of discovery, of finding the object and uncovering it for others to marvel at and speculate upon its story.

Her satnav speaks to her, instructing her to take the next turn and arrive at her destination. There's no mystery about her satnav. It is sometimes wrong; mostly it's right. But it's never mysterious; it's never ambiguous. And the only story it is concerned with is the linear journey from departure to arrival.

Its digital map even shows her the pond where the road turns sharply right. But it leaves things out: it doesn't show the five geese, standing at the roadside, like pedestrians waiting to cross.

As she drives slowly past them, her satnav tells her: 'You have reached your destination.'

She sees there's a small crowd already. And as she carefully parks her car beside the pond and climbs stiffly out onto the grass, she feels the old excitement rising in her.

What have they found?

99

*

There are two things to tell Dad when he gets back that afternoon – one very old and one very new. There's no doubt now about either of them. Both have been confirmed by experts. One is a new baby. The other is a Roman villa with a mosaic floor.

Poor Dad! Zara thinks. He's coming back from North Africa full of stories to tell us – tales about his brothers and sisters, his aunts and uncles, the houses they live in, the food they eat, the things that happen to them. *And he'll be so happy*, she thinks.

He doesn't know that *we* have the two best stories to tell *him*.

'But not till we get home,' Mum says. 'I don't want him making a great fuss at the railway station with all those people around! You know what he's like.'

So, back in their kitchen, the first news gets told.

'A *baby*?' he bellows. 'A *baby*?' He picks Mum up as if she were as light as a feather and whirls her round and round. Then there is a three-way hug in which Zara is enfolded with both of them. 'We mustn't squash the baby!' she says.

Dad kneels on the floor and puts his ear to Mum's stomach, as if he were eavesdropping on a conversation in the room next door. But he's too excited for silence. 'Hi! Baby!' he says. 'You in there! This is your father speaking!'

At that moment, old Mr Waller arrives to welcome Dad home.

Mr Waller has to be told about the baby, but it seems

to make him grumpy. He says he doesn't know anything about babies, never having had any. 'They're squishy objects, babies,' he says.

'You were one once,' Dad points out.

Mr Waller looks startled, as if he's doubtful. 'I s'pose I was,' he says. But he only half-believes it.

Then, when all four of them (five if you count the baby) are sitting round the table drinking coffee or juice, out comes the second story.

'A Roman mosaic?' Dad says slowly.

Zara nods eagerly. 'Yes!'

Dad looks at Mum for confirmation. This is hard to believe.

'That's what it seems to be,' Mum says. 'A Roman villa, with a mosaic floor.'

'And Zara found it?'

'Rob and me!' Zara says.

'We have them in North Africa too,' Dad says thoughtfully. 'Roman villas and Roman roads all over the place.'

'Who would've thought it?' Mr Waller says. 'They got everywhere, those Romans!'

Later, Mum and Dad and Zara set out on foot to Rob's farm to see the Roman site. 'Dad, can I ride on your shoulders?'

Mum and Dad laugh. 'You're a great lolloping schoolgirl, almost as tall as your father,' Mum says. 'You might as well suggest that he should give *me* a ride on his shoulders!'

It's true. But it's also sad, Zara reflects and half-wishes

that her dad *could* take her under the arms and hoist her high over his head and astride his shoulders. As if she were a three-year-old again, instead of a great lolloping schoolgirl.

She remembers how she loved it when she was little. There was a magic world up there, where she was higher than hedgerows and taller than trees, where hidden gardens became visible and tiny bedroom windows under thatches were almost within reach.

Now, she can recall the magic, but she can't recapture it. It's gone. *But I can still enjoy it*, she tells herself sensibly. The gardens are still there, and the little cottage windows.

'When I rode you on my shoulders, you used to pull your dress down over my face so that I couldn't see,' her father says. 'Or gouge my eyes out with your fingers. Or pull my hair out in tufts! When we got home, Mum had to glue my hair on and put my eyes back in.'

It's an old joke. 'Still,' Zara says to him severely, 'you need to get back in practice.'

*

People have started to arrive. It took just one phone call from Rob's mum. There is an archaeologist from Cambridge University, a research student from the UEA and a couple of experts from the County Council. A specialist from the British Museum is on his way.

Zara and Rob are allowed close because they were the people who found it. But the experts are watchful. The

Roman mosaic is theirs now, and soon it will be roped off and made secure.

At the bottom of the hole, neatly cleared and cleaned, is the mosaic bird. All of it. Most of its body is dark blue, and its legs are deep red. Its tail is twice as long as its body, gracefully drooping behind it. Its neck is bent like a swan's, its feathers shining. There are green leaves above and below it.

'A peacock,' one of the archaeologists explains. 'With its tail closed.'

But this bird has no eye. A single round stone is missing. The eye stone.

'And there's more of it,' says another. The experts have uncovered enough to show that this is only the corner of a big mosaic floor picture. The rest of it stretches away, still buried under the grass.

It's not perfectly flat. The picture is slightly wavy, with humps and hollows in it, as if a giant underneath had moved in his sleep through seventeen or eighteen centuries. And there are parts missing. But there is more to be discovered, more birds perhaps.

One of the archaeologists says: 'I'm Professor Barnes – Molly Barnes. Will you tell me how you found all this?'

She is very old. Zara's mum guesses she must be in her eighties, at least. Zara thinks she must be almost as old as David Attenborough. And she's still working as an archaeologist and a professor! Apparently, she's been on TV. Her face is serious but with tiny smile wrinkles around her eyes. Everyone treats her with great respect. Zara loses her voice as usual and takes a step back. But Rob tells the professor about the stones they found in the river and how they dug for more. 'Zara has a museum,' he says.

The professor studies Zara, but Zara says nothing, overwhelmed by her sudden importance. *Public* importance. All the words in her head have gone into hiding.

Rob asks a question. 'Why did the Romans go away and leave all their villas like that?'

'There were lots of reasons,' the professor says. 'The Roman empire was being attacked on all sides, even in Italy. And the emperor made an announcement that Rome could no longer protect Britain.'

'And they all left? Just like that?'

'Perhaps a few stayed, we're not really sure. And we don't know if they went straightaway. But most of them went, certainly.'

'And then what happened?'

'The Anglo-Saxons came,' Professor Barnes said. Then she added: 'Zara, I'm afraid I must ask to see the other things you found. May I come and see your collection?'

Dumbly, Zara nods.

*

Zara has been thinking about the story seller in the woods. 'We promised we'd tell him if we found anything,' she says later to Rob.

Rob agrees. So, back at Zara's house, they borrow Mum's laptop, which patiently allows them to search for the story seller's website.

It's full of his stories, and they are distracted for

several minutes. One is about a class of ten-year-olds who surprised their teacher by making a wildlife pond – filling it with water, stocking it with plants and adding tadpoles taken illegally from a nearby stream – and all without the teacher's knowledge. Another tells the story of a married couple who moved into a house and found in the attic two hundred stuffed birds in glass cases.

But the best story is about a blind man whose guide dog also went blind. For months the dog faithfully guided her master on all his familiar journeys, so successfully that no one suspected anything was wrong. But one day he set off by train to visit his sister in Manchester. At the railway station, the dog sat down and refused to take him on the train. Only then was the problem discovered and understood. The guide dog now lives in retirement and gets on well with the new dog. There is a picture of a handsome retriever, frowning a little, with puzzled eyes.

Zara types in the story seller's email address – *rovingstory@btinternet.com* – and they compose a message.

> *Hi! We've found a story for you. Do you remember us? We met you in the wood and told you about the orchids. And the milestone. You told us we should dig. Well, we did! And we've found a Roman mosaic floor. It's a bird, but it has no eye. It's great! But they won't allow us to do any more digging because we're not archaeologists.*
> *Bye!*
> *Rob and Zara.*

Zara adds a couple of kisses but Rob objects. '*I* don't want to send him kisses.' *Nor do I really*, Zara thinks. *It's only because I'm in a happy mood.*

'What about an emoji?'

Rob agrees to that.

So she deletes the kisses and the email is sent, with a grinning emoji instead.

Mum's computer sighs with pleasure as Zara sends it back to sleep.

A LOST TIME

They walk slowly, warily. A woman and two children, following at a small distance. All three are small.

Clothes? A few mean rags.

Boots? No, they're bare-footed.

Possessions? None that can be seen. They have nothing. Hardly any substance at all.

Where are they heading? Nowhere. Survival is their only destination.

The woman and the boy are sharp-eyed. But the girl's eyelids are clenched shut. She is sightless, led by her brother's hand.

The woman cries out. There's a bird on the ground, made of bright stones.

They crouch, staring. The blind girl – with her face raised to the sky, concentrating – feels around with her small, cold hands, brushing aside the dirt.

The boy finds a sharp flint. He pushes the point of it into the gummed-up space around the yellow eye stone. He works and pokes until the bird's eye comes loose. Then he picks it out and gives it to his blind sister. He wraps her cold fingers around it. Carefully, gently.

Now the bird is sightless, and the girl has one good eye.

Does he believe in magic? Probably just an instinctive reaching out for hope.

Who are they? They have no recorded place in time, no place anywhere. No one knows anything about them. Or cares.

And now they've gone, into the trees. And sixteen slow centuries have hidden them from our view.

We don't know their names, or the tribe they belonged to. Perhaps there was no tribe.

They are the true history of humankind. But we have forgotten them. They weren't difficult to forget.

Later, the girl probably lost faith in the yellow eye stone and dropped it.

Somewhere nearby.

Perhaps her eye got infected. And the infection spread, and she died.

Who knows?

17

THE FIRST TIME

Snow fell in the night-time, thick and freezing. My feet ploughed two snow ditches, ankle-deep. Hunger made me dizzy, my steps were unsteady. The thoughts in my head were scattered, like frightened birds.

The trackway went into a wood. It was dark in there. There was no sound. Branches and twigs were edged with snowfall. Every animal was still, every bird was in hiding. I felt them in my heart, clenched and crouched against the night cold, the winter frost.

Thin snowflakes fell through the tree roof. The wood was waiting. For daybreak, for spring, for five killers seeking.

A fox barked. I was alone, the fox was alone.

I thought of Guthlac and remembered the road in summer. A grassy highway through the wood, full of warm sounds and green shadows and bright flowers.

I had a dream picture. Guthlac floated above me, stern and angry. He held out his harp towards me. Then he was a fox, thin and hungry.

The dream picture broke. It was hunger madness.

There was another greenway crossing. A wide four-went-ways. There was no tree roof there, and the snow lay deeper, knee-high. Beyond it I saw flames in the trees, bright in the darkness, a fire blazing. Three wayfarers sat, warming themselves, wrapped in cloaks.

One stood upright and greeted me. His voice rang clear and frosty in the soft and soundless snow. There were two others, a woman and a young boy.

They told me their names: Brun, Edith and their son Aelfrith.

They welcomed me. I shivered by their fire. Around it there was mud and melted snow. But I would not sit. I would not stay. The thoughts in my mind ran wild, and only the need to reach my homestead was strong and clear in my heart.

'Five men?' I asked them. They shook their heads. No men had passed through the wood.

'They are killers and thieves,' I said.

Then the woman offered me food and drink.

My belly said yes but my thoughts were unsure. We heard men's voices coming near. They were behind, following. Nothing stood still; nothing was steady. The ground turned over, and the trees leaned.

I had passed the killers in the dark, unknowing. Or the wood had turned round, everything topsy-turvy.

The three travellers left their fire and drew back into

the trees. They had knives. Three people, three knives. The boy was young, a small, brave battle-companion. But hiding was their plan, and they vanished in the trees. They were wary and ready.

The woman ran after me. She pushed bread into my hand and folded my frozen fingers round it. 'Your homestead is westwards,' she said, pointing. Then she moved back into the darkness with her bondman and their son.

I stumbled on the track-way, a white road bending into distant trees. Wide, soundless, a way through the wood.

I looked back. The fire was a small spark afar, in the big darkness. Five twig-men drew near it. They stood in the open space of the four-went-ways. They waved their arms and pointed.

'Birds leave no footmarks. I will spread my wings and fly,' I said. My thoughts were adrift and astray.

But I did not fly. I stamped and stumbled through the deepening snow.

The wood turned sideways and upside down. I tore the woman's bread with my teeth and walked west.

18

THIS TIME AGAIN

Zara, alone in her room that night, gloomily thinking. Mum and Dad walking up and down outside, in the lane below, arm in arm, talking softly.

A baby in a belly, doing who knows what?

The smell of wallflowers drifting through Zara's open window.

The thrush in the top of Mr Waller's ash tree, singing in the warm darkness.

No stir of air is there, no movement of time.

The thrush's song is urgent, full of excitement and promise, but disciplined and correct. *Summer is coming! Come with me and we'll spend it together!* And because he has sung such perfect and joyous phrases, he repeats them twice, faultlessly. A deep, contented gurgle, followed by an ecstatic and free-flowing trill. Twice. And then a third time! Does he learn those phrases and practise them?

Zara's happy mood has not lasted, and now she's depressed and troubled. 'It's a teenager thing,' her mum said. 'Don't worry about it.'

Before her on the windowsill, she has arranged the Roman things, all intended for her museum. A few bits of broken clay pottery. *Boring!* The archaeologists are welcome to have them!

The half-bangle, made of rainbowy Roman glass. Yes, they can have that too.

The chunk of old mortar with part of the mosaic embedded in it. *I must give them that, I suppose,* she thinks.

But what about the seven stones she found in her bedroom years ago? Why should she have to give *them* away? She's had them almost all her life! She found them in her own bedroom, not at Rob's farm. Yet, it's clear that they belong to the mosaic floor.

She knows that one of the stones – the yellow round one – is the peacock's missing eye.

Forget those ancient objects! sings the thrush. *It's summer! Now! Now! Nothing else matters! Now is the time!*

And the bracelet of beads? In the warm darkness, its glassy colours are muted and shadowy, but Zara remembers how it shone when she washed it in the stream. She slips it over her left hand and settles it on her wrist, turning it round and round. *Who owned it?* she wonders for the hundredth time. Why was it placed under a brick? Who put it there? A woman? A girl?

Summer is coming. Don't waste time! Summer is almost here! Summer is here! Now! And I am master of everything I see!

A strange thought jumps into Zara's head from nowhere: *birdsong cannot lie,* she thinks. *It's impossible for a bird to tell lies.*

Why is Zara thinking about lies?

I can't bear to give this away, she thinks. *I won't tell them about it. We found it, not the archaeologists. And Rob said I could have all these things for my museum. He won't say anything.*

Everyone knows she hardly ever speaks. She will hide her secret inside her silence.

She hears the front door being shut as Mum and Dad come back inside. And, unexpectedly, the thrush falls silent in the darkness.

Where can I hide it?

*

Next morning there is a small crowd in Zara's back garden, most of them sitting around the big garden table in the flickering shade of the birch tree. Professor Barnes is there and the student assistant; Rob, too, with his dad; a man from the Chipping Walden Museum; and Zara.

Mum is in the kitchen, making coffee and stacking a large plate with biscuits. Her dad has gone to work, his first day back.

On the table are Zara's Roman finds. All except one.

'Let's start at the beginning,' the professor says. 'Tell me how you came to find these things.'

Zara ducks her head and looks sideways at Rob,

wordlessly passing the question to him with a desperate and slightly furtive look in her eye. Rob is used to this. He knows the signs. He tells a complicated but accurate story, prompted by questions. The student takes notes.

'Well, the blue poison bottle is history, but it's not *Roman* history,' Professor Barnes says. 'You may keep that. And the yo-yo and the rusty knife.'

'Poison?' Zara's mum says anxiously as she lowers a tray of coffee mugs onto the end of the table. 'Did you say *poison*?'

'Now, these bits of broken flowerpots. I'm afraid they are not flowerpots at all – they are fragments of Roman pottery. So we will have to take them too. They aren't worth anything, but they help us with dating.'

Zara doesn't care about the broken pottery. But her heart sinks because she knows what this means.

'And we must also take the fragment of a glass bangle, I'm afraid. We might eventually find the other half. That would be nice – it would have been a beautiful object. Now, these bits of mosaic…'

This is more difficult. Carefully, Rob explains that he found the chunk of fifteen stones in the river. 'But the other seven were in Zara's bedroom,' he says. 'She found them – *there*. Years ago.'

Still Zara says nothing.

'Where? How?'

This time it's Mum that Zara silently passes the question to. She does it by giving her a helpless look. 'They were in a crack between two floorboards,' Mum says.

'How did you come to find them?' the professor says.

This question is for Zara. There's no dodging it. 'A bouncy ball rolled under the radiator, and I was feeling around for it,' she says. But she speaks so quietly that no one hears what she says. So she has doubled her affliction because she now has to say it again, more loudly.

'Why should seven stones from a lost Roman villa appear in a house two miles away?' Professor Molly Barnes looks Zara straight in the eyes. Perhaps she is remembering how complicated the truth sometimes was in her own childhood.

Rob corrects her. 'One and a half,' he says.

No one has an answer for Professor Barnes' question. She is hesitant, not sure perhaps whether she has the right to take possession of the stones. They clearly belong to the mosaic, but they weren't found there.

'Is there anything else?' the professor asks.

Zara (wordless) shakes her head. She looks askance at Rob, seeking his support. Rob is loyal and usually willing to speak for her, but he won't be her lie-teller. He says nothing about the beaded bracelet.

At that moment, two things happen almost simultaneously. First, Mr Waller's thrush starts to sing from the chimney stack on the roof. Only Zara notices. Second, her mum's phone bursts into a busy piece of Vivaldi, and Mum – looking embarrassed and apologetic – walks a few steps from the rest so that she can take the call. They all pretend they're not listening.

'What? Who? Are you sure? *Really? Are you sure?*'

She stares at Rob and Zara. 'That was Rob's mum,' she says. 'Apparently there's a man at the farm. He says his name is Roving Story or something, and you two are friends of his!'

'He says he knows you too,' she adds, speaking to the professor.

Professor Barnes groans. 'Oh, *no!* Him! That means the place will be crawling with media people within hours! We must get back!'

*

But not Zara. She wants to be alone. Twice Rob has texted her to tell her to come to his house. But for the rest of the morning and all afternoon, she has ignored him. And his messages. Her phone is switched off.

This is a new, secretive Zara. Sitting alone under the birch tree in her back garden, she considers the glass beads. *I can't bear to give them up,* she tells herself.

The morning visitors have gone, and Mum is back at work at her computer. Zara is seized by a longing to know the past – the Roman past – and an exciting thought has come to her. Perhaps the bracelet can unite her with the person who once owned it.

Her heart quickens. She has read about such things. In stories.

The bracelet's owner was a girl probably, sad because she'd lost it. But that's as far as ordinary thinking can take Zara.

She needs a different kind of thought.

She slips the bracelet over her wrist. Perhaps a rare and mysterious time magic will take possession of her and, with perfect safety, wrap her whole being in the past. Not time travel, she knows that's impossible. And, anyway, she'd be too scared to go in case she never gets back. But a special kind of vivid clarity might appear in her mind – a message, or a picture of a scene perhaps. A private link across fifteen or sixteen centuries, like the connection between her phone and Rob's.

How lovely it would be if she could *see* the original owner of the bracelet and talk to her. A magical kind of Zoom, or Skype.

Leaning back, she concentrates – hard – taking deep, slow breaths and relaxing her upper body. She knows how to do this because she has been taught to do it for diving competitions. Her breathing deepens; her heart slows; and her mind opens and spreads like a flower, focusing all her sensations.

Will it happen?

She concentrates on the bangle and the unknown girl from the past who once owned it. Was she a Roman? How old was she? What colour was her hair? Her eyes? Her skin? ('They were a multicoloured lot, those Romans,' Mr Waller would say. 'They came from all over.') Was she beautiful and tall? Or small and half-starved? Or strong and warrior-like, perhaps? How did she come to lose her bracelet? Or had she deliberately hidden it under the floor brick? And if so, *why?*

Zara, with eyes closed and a frown of concentration on her brow, waits for a moment of magic, a vision of knowledge so sharp and pure that all her questions will be answered.

But no answers come. Instead, slipping stealthily into her mind are the now sounds around her – a distant tractor, a car accelerating up the hill and a cuckoo, the first one this year! – echoing afar across the valley. Then, from closer at hand, she hears Mum in the kitchen, shutting a cupboard door. Finally – from even closer – her own body breathing, the soft sound of air drawn in and out and the insistent quiet pulse of her heartbeat.

It's not the past she has been taken to, it's back to the present.

Disappointed, she opens her eyes and looks down at the beaded bracelet, bright against the soft, lighter skin on the tender underside of her wrist. They are just glass beads from long ago, that's all. Very old but possessing no time magic.

A new sound is added. A robin, on a branch of the birch tree and only a few feet from Zara, catches her eye and sings. A few brief, piercing notes, almost beyond the reach of her hearing.

Then, in the wink of an eye, the song is done, and the bird has gone, and Zara has her moment of understanding. But it's not what she'd hoped for. What she understands is that she can think about the past, read about it, Google it, dig for it and, above all, *imagine* it. But she can't ever fully know it. It is irretrievable. Gone!

It's always *once* upon a time. Not over and over again. Not even twice. Just *once*.

She slips the bracelet over her hand and knows exactly what she must do with it. As she does so, she thinks – she has no idea why – about the coming baby. And the way that Mum sometimes rests her hand on her stomach, taking care of the future.

She runs indoors. 'Mum! I'm going to Rob's! OK?'

Then she's off like a rocket! Before her mum can say anything.

19

ANOTHER TIME

All journeys end.

Thomas rounds the final bend and is able at last to see the lights of home at the bottom of the hill. In the warm summer darkness, a man is standing in the lane.

He waves his arms and raises his voice in a cry of welcome.

'Father!' Thomas shouts.

Up the hill comes Father in seven-league strides. He grabs Rob's spare hand and shakes it, man to man. 'I'm glad you're home,' he says. 'Well done.'

Uncle William, leaning over the wrong hedge, greets them.

'Did you go through Howe's Wood, like I said?'

'I kept to the road.'

'You're a cautious one!'

'Are you worn out?' Father asks.

'*Hungry!*'

In the wrong kitchen, Aunt Meg cuts a slice of the right cake and fills a tankard with fresh cow's milk.

'Did you find the Banbury man?'

'Did you buy any books?'

'Did you fall foul of Old Lopsy?'

'How did you get those sticks?'

'Where's Mother?'

'She's in bed, son.'

'Is she ill?'

'Go and see.'

He finds enough energy for climbing the narrow stairs and lifting the iron latch of the bedchamber.

There – pink-faced and glowing softly in candlelight – Mother lies back amid pillows. She smiles and holds out her arms.

The traveller and the traveller's mother hug one another.

'Why are you in bed? Why are aunt and uncle in our house? Why didn't Father go haymaking today?'

'Well—'

'And why did you send me away?'

'See!'

Beside her on the bed is the deep bottom drawer from the bow-fronted chest on the landing. In it (bundled in woollen shawls) are two new babies. One has tiny blue eyelids frowningly shut. The other quietly watches itself, gently wrestling with fistfuls of air.

'Are they ours?'

'Yes. This one is a girl and this one is a boy. No, that's

wrong! It's the other way round.'

'Babes in a box.'

Why hadn't he realised? He knows about babies, and he'd observed his mother's big belly. But casually. He hadn't worked it out.

'Did you get my scissors?'

'Yes.'

'And *Cock Robin*?'

'Yes.'

'And lots of others?'

'Yes! Yes!'

Father, standing in the doorway, says, 'Did you get *The Fair Rosamond*?'

'The Banbury man didn't have her.'

'Well, did you get *Babes in the Wood*?'

'Yes, but you were wrong, Father! *They didn't die!*'

'They *did*! And the birds covered their bodies with dead leaves. Everyone knows that story.'

But Thomas is triumphantly right. 'I've got another book which tells how they were found alive. By a good man called Honestas.'

'Alive and well?'

'Yes.'

'Astonishing!' Father says.

'Father, I met the hedge cutter, and he made me buy him some bawdy.'

'Did he now?'

'And he cut me three sticks.'

'One big one for you,' Father says, 'and two small twin-sticks.'

Mother and Father look at one another. 'I wonder how he knew,' Mother says.

Downstairs, Thomas sits at the kitchen table, feeling manly. Aunt Meg's movements flutter the candle flame as she serves supper.

'Time for bed,' she says.

'I would quite like to be a Banbury giant.'

'Is that so? All that travelling?'

'Aunt Meg, may I have a candle?'

'Bed is for sleep, not reading.'

Father leans in at the window, smelling of broad beans. 'Let the boy have a candle, Meg. Just for tonight. To read by.'

*

Down in the moonlit lane, Aunt Meg and Uncle William set off back to their cottage. Their voices can be heard as they slowly climb the hill.

The seven flat stones are laid out on the windowsill, lit by moonlight. Four of them are pale blue, two are mottled green. But one of them is round – flat like the others – bright and yellow, like stony marmalade.

Where, thinks Thomas, did they come from? Was Old Lopsy right – did they really grow in the ground like potatoes?

The round eye stares upwards, flat and pale in the moonlight.

Afterwards, in a cave of candlelight under the sloping ceiling, Thomas reads the Banbury books. Then the candle flame is blown out and pale moonlight comes into the room.

Under the coverlet, his thoughts go back to the first of the stories. Then, half asleep, they go back to the start of the day. Finally, in dreams, they go back to lost and forgotten beginnings, where old things have their stories.

Six of the flat stones are arranged in a row on the window ledge. But the seventh – the round one – is in Thomas's hand, clasped tight in sleep.

20

THIS TIME

Freewheeling down the hill towards Rob's house, Zara takes in the scene.

An enclosed van as big as a bus has been reversed carefully into the space beside Rob's pond. It has "BBC" in big letters on the side. There is a small crowd of people – people with clipboards, people wearing earphones, people with tablets, some just standing around, waiting. There are cameras held on shoulders, monitors and screens and fur-covered microphones on long booms.

The experts are standing apart from this busy confusion, close to the uncovered mosaic, polite and cheerful but clearly guarding it.

Zara leans her bike against the hedge and watches for a few moments. Rob comes out of his house and sees her. Loyal as always, he hurries across.

'Why didn't you answer my texts?'

He sees she is wearing the bracelet. 'Will you come with me?' Zara says. There's no need to explain; he understands at once.

They approach the group of experts where Professor Barnes is standing. For a few awkward moments, the two children are ignored. But Rob lightly touches the professor's sleeve to attract her attention. She is bent in her old age, stooping, smaller than the two young people standing beside her.

Zara is very struck by this, that the professor has to look *up* to them.

'We found this too,' she says. She holds out her left arm.

The professor takes Zara's wrist as if she were a doctor measuring her pulse. Slowly, she moves the bracelet round so that she can see each of the beads against Zara's skin. Amber, coloured glass and bone.

'Isn't it lovely?' she says. 'But it's not Roman.' To one of her colleagues, she says: 'Look – look at this!'

'This is Anglo-Saxon,' the professor says to Zara. 'And you found it in a Roman villa?'

The other experts lean in, wanting to look closely at Zara's wrist.

'Anglo-Saxon women liked beads – they pinned them on their dresses, mostly,' Professor Barnes explains. 'Hanging straight down. But beaded bracelets are found from time to time too.'

'But this one was close beside a Roman mosaic,' Rob says.

'There's some doubt,' the professor says, 'about whether

the Anglo-Saxons moved into the Roman buildings after the Romans had left. Well, one of them must have lived here or visited.'

Heads are bent and backs stooped over Zara's extended arm.

'I'm not surprised,' Professor Barnes says carefully, 'that you wanted to hang onto it for a little longer.'

Then Zara understands that no more needs to be said. Her guilty secret has popped and vanished like a burst bubble on a sunny day.

'May I?' the professor asks and makes a move to take off the bracelet. But Zara draws back her wrist and removes it herself. Then she hands it over.

Professor Barnes smiles. It's a secret smile, an eye-to-eye smile. It's a smile that comes from within, and it has nothing to do with archaeology or history. It is an old woman and a much younger one understanding each other, fleetingly.

'It's *beautiful*!'

'In a Roman villa?'

'Interesting!'

'Late fifth century, at a guess, wouldn't you say? Or early sixth?'

'Zara, can you show us where you found it?' Professor Barnes says.

But it's Rob who shows them where the beaded bracelet was found, buried under a floor brick. This is not because Zara has become shy and speechless again. It's because this busy crowd of noisy and confident people have driven the Anglo-Saxon girl away. She once owned the beads – and loved them and wore them and hid them and lived her own life – but now she seems suddenly to have faded and receded, diminished into an impossible distant past as if she'd never existed at all, leaving Zara feeling lost and sad.

But Rob, beside her, softly presses his foot on hers and leans slightly against her shoulder. Zara's tiny pang of sadness goes away.

There is a shout. 'Ah! *There* you are!'

It is the story-seller, rovingstory.himself.com! He has spotted them and is limping towards them. 'I've been looking for you. Well, you two have certainly done it! Now, tell me all about it.'

But there's no time for storytelling. The professor is coming back to them, holding out her hand. In it are the stones that were, until this morning, part of Zara's museum: four blue, two green and a round one the colour of marmalade.

'We don't yet know where these six belong,' she says, 'but we *do* know where the round one should go. It needs to be in its proper place, and we'd like you to put it there.'

The confusion of people becomes an audience, closing in, gathering round, intent on seeing – and filming – what is going to happen.

'I have a granddaughter rather like you,' Professor Barnes says as they walk across to the uncovered mosaic. She tucks her hand through Zara's arm. Zara likes this, but she finds it a little embarrassing.

A small part of the floor picture has been properly brushed and gently cleaned by the archaeologists, and the hole where the peacock ought to have an eye has been neatly scoured and emptied of the hard, dry earth that had become encrusted in it.

What is going to happen is improper procedure. But no one, seeing that hole – and knowing there's a stone that fits it – could fail to want the pictured bird restored to completeness. Just for a few moments. Not even professional archaeologists.

'Take your shoes off,' the professor says.

So Rob and Zara, in their socks, step onto the mosaic. 'You do it,' Zara whispers to Rob. 'No,' he says firmly. 'It's your stone.'

Zara kneels on the mosaic. The lemon-yellow eye stone is not a perfect circle. She has to adjust it, to settle it snugly in its socket.

Perfect fit! she thinks.

The peacock has its eye again. And for some illogical reason, everyone cheers and claps. More photographs are taken: two strapping teenagers, with the tiny octogenarian archaeologist standing between them.

*

But what is going to happen next has no reason that Rob and Zara can see. There's an unexpected coming-together of everyone, a drifting towards the centre, a focusing, like disturbed bees gathering around their queen. No one explains; no one gives an order. With a single mind, everyone draws closer, and conversations grow hushed and finally fall quiet. It's like that moment at a wedding, when the congregation falls silent knowing the bride is about to enter.

What is happening? Zara thinks. She and Rob exchange puzzled glances.

No one explains, no one asks permission. A nice-looking young man called Monty manoeuvres them into a place where he wants them to stand and says to them, 'I want you to look there when you answer my questions. *There!*'

Complete silence now. Zara, mystified, observes that everyone is paying attention to a few small screens. Not just paying attention but rapt, concentrating and clearly *waiting*. With a shock, she realises that what she can see on the big screen is the six o'clock news, and there is a man telling them about a politician who has misbehaved.

Then, with a sudden sinking of the heart, she understands what's coming. And she knows she can't do it. It's impossible. Her heart is racing, anticipating fear.

A man with headphones raises his hand, pointing. There is complete silence. The news presenter on the screens says: 'Two children in north Essex have uncovered what, at first sight, seems to be a Roman villa with a floor mosaic. Over now to our *Look East* correspondent, Montgomery Wise. Monty—'

'Hugh!' says Monty. Zara can hear him twice, his ordinary voice and an electronic version of it, simultaneously.

After a short introduction, Monty turns to Rob and begins to question him. He has probably been told, Zara thinks, that the girl is always tongue-tied, and he'd do better with the boy.

But Rob isn't very good at this. He's not tongue-tied, and he can answer all the questions, but Monty asks him the wrong kind of question. 'What did you feel,' he says, 'when you first saw the mosaic?'

Rob thinks this is a waste of everyone's time. And a waste of words. What have his feelings got to do with it?

So the interviewer gives him a prompt. 'Did you feel *excited*?'

'Yes,' Rob says, 'but I was also puzzled—'

Monty interrupts him. 'How pleased are you to have made such a notable contribution to history?'

Rob thinks this is one of the stupidest questions anyone could possibly ask. 'I don't believe,' he says truthfully, 'I ever thought about making a contribution to history.'

People bite their lower lips, trying not to laugh. Monty never was any good at interviewing kids!

Monty turns to Zara. He glances down quickly to check her name and says, 'Zaira? No, Zara! Tell us how you came to make this remarkable discovery.'

Astonishingly, Zara is filled with an unexpected and exhilarating determination to *tell the story*. She half-understands there are several million viewers watching her. Yet her shyness has miraculously vanished, and she's not tongue-tied at all. This story has to be told. So she begins. And the words inside her head have lost their shyness and come pouring out, in the right order and making sense.

Where has this new-found confidence come from? Is it perhaps because Mr rovingstory.com at that moment gives her an encouraging wink?

Or is it because she wants to help out Rob? Or because there is no escape, and she simply *has* to do it?

Or perhaps it's her liberation from guilt, the release from her secret. Perhaps she is like the princess in the story, who, despite the fact that she slept on twenty mattresses, was still made uncomfortable by a single dried pea underneath them all. The pea that troubled Zara is no longer there. Her small private shame has been disposed of.

Zara thinks it's because there are people standing around her, and they're excited and interested. The very air is charged with curiosity. And Professor Barnes is watching her, attentive and wanting to know. They *all* want to know, and she's the only one who can explain it to them.

Above all, she aches to tell them how truly *beautiful* the bracelet is! *And I love it so much!*

'Well,' she says firmly, 'Rob found the first stones. He's my best friend. He found them in the stream over there. And when we found the bracelet, it was full of lovely colours...'

In her kitchen at home, Zara's mum – after a long day's work – switches on the television in the kitchen and is beginning to think about the evening meal. She has paid little attention to the first items on the six o'clock news, but suddenly she concentrates and stares at the screen.

'Good lord!'

She sits down heavily onto a chair, probably giving

a mild shock to the baby living temporarily inside her. She stares in disbelief at her daughter, on television, explaining to the nation how she and Rob came to uncover a completely unknown Roman villa.

'Zara!' she whispers to herself. 'Oh, Zara!'

How grown-up she looks!

Zara has told the story clearly and briefly. The viewers are given a quick close-up of the mosaic bird; the interviewer asks Rob one last question and finally turns to Professor Barnes and asks her a few too.

Then: 'Back to you in the studio, Hugh.'

That seems to be the signal. They are no longer on air, and there is a huge and disorderly hubbub, an immediate outburst of talk, like the clamour of starlings.

But it's short-lived, for Monty tells them they are going to have to repeat it almost immediately for another item on the local news programme, *Look East*. This will be longer, with close-ups and more shots of the mosaic bird. With its yellow eye back in place.

OK, thinks Zara, *that's fine!* She is excited, fired – she *wants* to do it all again. She has found her tongue and heard her voice.

This time, Monty asks her about the bird's missing eye. *I must be careful*, Zara thinks. It would take too long to explain that she'd found this stone in her bedroom. Listeners would be distracted and puzzled. She knows instinctively that this detail is part of the full story but not part of the TV version. 'One of the stones we had was a yellow round one,' she says. 'And it goes in the space where the peacock's eye was missing. It's a perfect fit.'

There's another close-up of the bird, with its marmalade eye in position. It's different from the rest because there is no Roman mortar holding it in place.

'Is it true,' Monty asks Professor Barnes, 'that there have also been some Anglo-Saxon finds?'

'Yes – well one, at least. The bracelet that Zara and Rob found is Anglo-Saxon.'

'Does this mean that Anglo-Saxons lived in the half-ruined Roman dwellings?'

Monty's good on context, the bystanders think. He's hopeless with children but he likes to get the history right.

However, the professor will not give a clear answer. 'That's a good question,' she says. 'But the truth is that we don't know.'

And then it's all over, and Zara sees Mum parking the car out in the road. She slams the door and hurries across the grass and through the crowd.

When she has finished hugging Zara and Rob (she always hugs Rob too), they tell her she missed the second interview. 'It will be repeated later,' someone explains. 'After the ten o'clock news.'

'Dad will be home from work,' Zara says happily.

*

Professor Barnes, driving home later, pulls into a gateway leading into a yellow field. She opens the window and savours the cool air of a summer evening and the sharp, mustard smell of oilseed rape.

The silence enfolds her, and unaccountably, she is

taken back to another summer, 1945, the year the war ended. And she thinks of Adam and Abigail, her lifelong lover and her lifelong friend. We were sixteen that year, she recalls.

She remembers the mere on the edge of the town, *their* mere. Too big for a pond, not large enough for a lake. It was secret and hidden – no one ever went there or even knew about it. On hot days that summer, the three of them swam and dived and swam again and spread themselves out to dry and warm up in the sun. They took swimsuits, for form's sake, but they never bothered with them.

She is taken aback by these memories unexpectedly washing over her: the discreet puddling of a nearby family of ducks and ducklings, the smell and sound of rain on the surface of the lake (it did rain a couple of times that summer, she recalls), the sweet, soft mud under their feet as they pushed out into deeper water. And the feel of the tender, grassy bank when at last they swam back and climbed out to lie on their towels.

They've both gone now. And when I'm gone too, she thinks, all these memories – intimate, sensual, heartbreaking glimpses of her lovely, private worldful – will die too. And no one will ever know. Every life on earth, she thinks, finally submits to this ultimate vanishing. Eighty-odd years of memories, a trillion-fold, will lose their fragile grasp, switched finally off.

Beyond recovery, beyond the reach of historians and archaeologists, beyond all possible uncovering. Gone. Just gone.

Lost in time.

But strangely, she feels comforted. It's those two, she thinks. Zara and Rob. They set me off thinking about that summer. She always finds young people consoling. They know very little about it – they're not even interested – and yet they have the power to cheer and to heal.

Rob and Zara, she thinks. He stalwart and faithful, she something of a mystery, beginning to unfold.

21

THE FIRST TIME

Through thick, falling flakes, I saw the lights of my homestead. I made eager speed, but my feet stumbled in deep snow. At the gate there were warriors guarding, hugging themselves in the frosty wind, stamping their feet like horses.

I shouted, 'I am Sæwara!'

A boy warrior shouted – he was a youngling with older men. It was Eadweard.

He ran to meet me through the thickening snow. Our greeting was seemly, we hid our joy.

Wulfstan came, the grim reeve. 'Where is Guthlac?'

I told them Guthlac the story-teller was dead, murdered by thieves. Then their hearts were filled with grief. Men vowed vengeance. They pulled their knives from under their cloaks and set off into the darkness and the falling snow.

'Come!' the reeve said. 'You must come to the mead-hall. There is food and feasting, and our battle lord, your mother's brother, awaits you.'

Then Eadweard spoke: 'Sæwara must wash and comb her hair and put on a bright kirtle and gown.'

I knew the heart that was in him. He spoke with sternness before older men. But I laid my frozen hand on his arm. 'I am a traveller,' I said. 'I must not come before our battle lord dressed and decked like a bridal maid.'

He went with me inside the fence, and we crossed the yard. The houses crouched, humped and hushed in the sweeping, swooping snow. A child's face, like a small moon, watched from a half-open door.

This was my home, my safe place.

Inside the high-gabled hall, there was loud laughter and feasting – men, women, children and dogs – and on his high seat, the chieftain sat, the battle-lord, the gift-giver. Heat and smoke made me faint, shouting warriors stunned my thinking. But Eadweard held me upright with his strong arm. He led me to the chieftain, my mother's brother, giver of gifts and protector of men.

The king raised his right hand, and there was quietness in the hall. 'Sæwara, welcome home!' he said. 'But where is Guthlac? He took you with him, but you have come home alone. Where is Guthlac, the brave minstrel, our story-singer?'

'He is dead, sir.'

Then there were cries of grief and wonder. A great clamour. The reeve raised his voice in sorrow. 'Weep! Weep for Guthlac! What will we do for stories? Who will sing us our songs? Guthlac was full of years, and he held our history. He sang of battles and journeys across the perilous whale-road and told us of our great heroes, our brave grandfathers and grandmothers who once walked in middle-earth.'

That is the way of my people. We are good at grief.

Then the reeve fell quiet and the king, my foster father, watched me. His eyes were my eyes; his brow was my brow; under his beard, his mouth and chin were mine. He was my mother's brother. He knew the longing of my heart.

'Now,' said the king, 'you must eat and drink. Eadweard, fetch food and wine for Sæwara the wayfarer! Make a seat for her close to the fire.'

Then Swanhild, the queen, with jewelled necklet and bright gold on her white breast, walked among the warriors at the mead-benches, cheering their hearts. Her handmaidens went with her, carrying the golden mead-flagon, filling goblets.

Swanhild was as straight as a young tree and as fair as a bird singing at sunrise. Swanhild the brave, who had fought in battle beside the king, many times.

She came to me and spoke. 'Sæwara, our loved one, there is a battle in my heart. Sorrow for Guthlac, the brave story-teller, wrestles with joy that my husband's sister-daughter has come safely home.'

Swanhild was like a young birch tree in spring sunshine.

In the darkness of the rafters above the heads of my kinsfolk, I saw a small brown bird, a sparrow entering the hall, unseen in the shadowy roof beams. It flew across the hall through smoke and gloom, in at one end and out at the other. Then it was gone, the small bird, into the howling, bitter night. As it flitted above me, I saw its eye, bright and quick. It knew me, and I knew it.

I thought of Juliana, child of the old ones, the last of an unknown tribe, fearless in winter in her thatched house, like a small, brown mouse in her nest. Where, I thought, will she hide my treasure gift?

When my belly was full and my heart was cheered, the king spoke. The hall fell quiet. 'Sæwara!' he said. 'Guthlac brought our stories with us, from the old countries. Now it is you who must sing us the story of his death, the brave world-traveller, the way-wanderer.'

There was silence in the great hall. The warriors were still. Outside, the blizzard roared, the winter-dragon. The thick thatch stirred and creaked in the wind, and the oak walls groaned.

'The harp is Guthlac's,' I said. 'I cannot play.'

'You will learn,' the king said. 'The harp is yours. But now, this night, let your words tell us how Guthlac died, our brave minstrel and story-teller.'

I was a woman. I looked at Eadweard. His eyes were wide.

Then Swanhild spoke. 'As a dragon guards its treasure, so Guthlac guarded his story hoard. Sæwara, now you must unlock your word chest and tell us your story. Your story is his story. Stories are for telling. So, tell us of your journey with Guthlac, of your visit to the mead-hall of the brave over-king, the great sea-king in the east. Tell us how

Guthlac went to his long home in the lower world and how you came safely back in blast and blizzard.

'I will,' I said.

Eadweard stood beside me. 'Have you courage?' he said. 'For story-telling?'

'Yes. I will honour Guthlac, whose spirit wanders the lower world.'

But Wulfstan the reeve spoke. There was sternness in his words. 'Story-telling is for *men*.'

Swanhild gave him his answer. 'Story-telling is for the story-teller,' she said. 'Our story-teller is Sæwara.'

A picture was in my thoughts. Our songs and stories still feel unwelcome and strange in this new land. But in time they will wrap around the trunks of trees and make themselves at home here. They will hold us and tell us who our neighbours are. They will tell us about brave warriors and loyal companions. Sometimes they will snarl and sneer and snap. Sometimes they'll grow comfortable and curl up under summer hedgerows. Yes, and they will tell us about cooking too, about chicken legs and cheese. And children.

I stood. 'I have a riddle,' I said. 'For Guthlac.' There was silence in the hall.

I am a story-storer
tale-teller
way-walker
country-crosser
dragon-dreamer
mead-master...

There was laughter in the hall. Someone called out: 'He liked his mead, Guthlac did! But *it* mastered *him*!'

> *…memory-maker*
> *dream-drawer*
> *stream-stepper*
> *hill-strider*
> *word-weaver.*

Then the warriors and women in the hall stamped their feet on the wooden floor, and the king smiled. Queen Swanhild's eyes shone.

Then the words walked from my mouth. The spirit of Guthlac was in my heart. But they were *my* words, orderly and clear. In the smoke of the hall, I made bright pictures for my kinsfolk. The king and Swanhild the fair, and the women and warriors in the hall, saw before their eyes the five robbers and the fall of Guthlac in the fire smoke. Children knelt on the floor, story-bound, watching my face. They saw his death and the chase through the wood. The Roman ghost house, place of spirits, gave them terror in the darkness. They saw Juliana the fearless, and the treasure gift I gave her, and they wondered in their hearts.

I was a girl-woman. I was their story maker. I stood tall.

*

In the place of honour I slept, Sæwara the story-teller, wrapped in fur skins, close to the fire. I woke in the deep hours after midnight and heard the rough breathing of warriors sleeping in the hall. Red-hot embers settled softly in the ashes of the fire.

The king, my uncle, and Swanhild, the queen, slept in their bed place.

I heard men shouting.

In the yard outside, there was the movement of warriors, a loud challenge and an answer. The great door of the hall crashed open.

Men were startled in their sleep, sitting up, grabbing their knives. The king's curtain was swept aside. Beside me, Eadweard leapt to his feet. His knife was in his right hand, a thick wooden shield in his left.

A band of warriors, bringing with them the bitter night air, came boldly into the hall. They spilt snow. Four of them carried a corpse, a long body. I saw his grey face as they drew near and knew him. He was the leader, the Guthlac-killer. He had followed me from far away, over the empty hills. I had known his thoughts and his lust. They dropped the body on the floor at the king's feet. It thumped on the wooden boards and settled. 'He has paid the death-price,' one of the warriors said.

It was our way.

The king stepped down and greeted his warriors. 'Guthlac's spirit can rest now,' he said. 'He was far-famed in this world. Now, in the lower world, he can walk in pride.'

He stooped and took the golden pin that held the killer's cloak. 'This was Guthlac's brooch,' he said. 'Sæwara, it is yours now. Your first king's gift.'

The four murder-companions were brought forward. Their faces were grey and grim, their hands were tied with rope, and they staggered, almost falling. The king spoke: 'Take them to the slave house.'

There was silence again in the great hall when the warriors left, taking away the dead man and the four captives. Queen Swanhild, lovely in sleep, came to me. She held a thick wrap around her shoulders against the night cold. 'Sæwara, you are safe now. And Guthlac is avenged. The Guthlac-killer and his henchmen cannot hurt you.'

But sleep would not come back. I started a riddle about story-tellers.

We make things which are not there.
We know when to begin and when to stop...

22

THIS TIME

Molly Barnes, seated at last in her darkening garden, with a bedtime glass of milk and three digestive biscuits, remembers 1945. She's tired and thoughtful. On her lap is a drawing, done by Adam on the afternoon following VJ Day. It's normally kept in a folder, privately, among her papers.

She and Adam were sixteen that year. Abigail too. And everything changed.

Adam is famous now. So she knows that after her death, the drawing will be exposed to the public eye and will become the centre of a great deal of attention.

Her thoughts go back to the street party in their town, celebrating victory over Japan, the absolute and final end of World War Two. They'd danced and sung and partied all night, the whole town, mostly in the streets and in other people's gardens.

She's taken aback by the power of the past. She'd thought that August 1945 was safely tucked away and lost in the distance of more than seventy years gone, but it isn't. It's close at hand, under her breast, inside her heart.

None of us went to bed that night.

They'd danced in the streets and listened to records on gramophones. Someone had dragged the primary school piano out into the playground, and a crowd quickly gathered. There was an endless sing-along, under the stars, simultaneously joyous and sorrowful – *You Are my Sunshine, Pack Up Your Troubles* and that faithful old tear-jerker, *We'll Meet Again.* They'd danced and chatted to friends, visited houses and back gardens where they'd never been before, and the long summer twilight turned imperceptibly into dawn.

But the next day, everyone was exhausted. And by the afternoon, the whole town was asleep.

They returned to the guest house, just the two of them, she recalls. Abigail had gone off somewhere. Everyone in the town seemed to have found a place to sleep.

The past floods over her, like an enchantment, filling her with longing.

They found the back door wide open and the house silent, she remembers. The afternoon warmth poured quietly indoors, among the shadows. It was always like that on warm afternoons, when the house was empty. She'd wondered briefly where her mum was.

Quietly, she and Adam went upstairs. There was no one else in the whole world.

On the top floor, under the roof, was a room used

for storing unwanted furniture and bedding. Beside the window stood a spare bed, and against another wall there was a small stack of mattresses, along with pillows and folded blankets. When she was small, she used to pretend a little old woman lived up there with her spinning wheel, waiting cheerfully to cast her spell on anyone who entered.

Adam had turned up in her life as an evacuee, in 1940, aged eleven, bringing with him his drawing materials and his talent. He sometimes worked in this room. The window faced north, and there was a skylight in the roof so that the light in the room was clear and shadowless.

Molly, dazed with tiredness, kicked off her sandals, grabbed a pillow and lay back on the narrow bed. *He stood for a moment, looking down at me*, she remembers.

'Will you take your things off?'

Molly frowned briefly, wanting to sleep.

But she wasn't wearing much. So she sat up, unbuttoned her blouse and slipped it off, along with her bra. Then she raised her hips and shuffled down her skirt and knickers as far as her knees. It was left to Adam to pull the garments clear of her feet and drop them on the floor. She lay back and closed her eyes, and her last conscious memory was the touch of his hands on her skin as he pulled the garments clear of her feet.

She dropped swiftly into sleep as he turned away to find sketchbook, charcoal and pencils.

He sketched her while she slept. She lay with her left hand raised to her head and her right lying alongside her body. He drew the fingers of her right hand a little longer than they really were, her hips a little wider, her thighs a little fuller, her pubic hair thicker and more tangled. Her upper body – her small breasts, shoulders and throat and face – had a firmness and grace of line that other artists later came to envy and admire. Finally, he rubbed his fingertip over her hair to smudge it a little.

He'd drawn her as if she were twenty-six. But he was an accurate and uncanny predictor. *It took me ten years*, she recalls, *to catch up*.

Only last year, a researcher cataloguing all Adam Swales' works (a hopeless task) had questioned whether the drawing should be listed as a nude or a portrait. He'd written that it was made "with a respectful and tender lust".

Respectful? Molly wonders – yes!

Tender? Always!

Lust? She smiles inwardly with an immense and complex sadness.

She'd slept for around a couple of hours. She remembers waking to the sound of soft footsteps on the stairs. The door was pushed softly open and Abigail tiptoed in. Adam lay on the pile of mattresses, asleep. On the bed lay Molly, naked as a needle.

Molly opened her eyes as Abigail walked softly across to the table where Adam kept his drawing things. She picked up the sketch and studied it. '*Crikey!*' she said.

Memory, memory, Molly thinks. *Getting up to its old tricks!* But a little of that afternoon, she tells herself now, will endure in spite of time. In Adam's drawing.

For a century or two, anyway. If the world gets lucky.

Later, Adam added his monogram. He named the sketch simply *Molly Sleeping*.

In time, she thinks, *half the world will come to love it, buy reproductions of it, tea towels, table mats.*

*

On a bright, sunny morning, Mr Reeve stands in the doorway of his antique shop and surveys the activity in the market square.

He likes market days. There are people everywhere, young and old and in-between. People buying, people queuing, people chatting. Tall, purposeful people with shopping bags, small, bored people in buggies, people with wonky hips, people looking at their phones. And a lean and skinny boy in a dark hood, glaring. There are stalls selling cheeses, stalls selling clothes and stalls selling herbs, knick-knacks, fresh fish, fruit and veg and one selling tools which are so old that only very old people remember how to use them. There are voices shouting, greeting, grumbling, laughing. And a hard-up couple by the cash machine, anxiously studying a statement to see if they can afford to withdraw five pounds.

Mr Reeve, taking it all in, notices out of the corner of his eye a boy and a girl approaching his shop window. *Where have I seen that girl's face before?* he asks himself.

'There!' Rob says, pointing.

Zara stares.

In pride of place in Mr Reeve's window display, along with a pair of Edwardian silk gloves and a silver jewellery box, stands her longed-for metal bird. But its cage is no longer rusty and dirty. The thin, vertical bars have been cleaned and rubbed smooth and painted gold. The bird, too, is no longer entirely shabby. One wing has been cleaned to reveal its long-lost brightness and colour: a crisp, summery apple-green and yellow, hinting at the loveliness of the rest, still hidden under layers of grime.

Beside it there is a notice: "FOR RESTORATION £50".

'*£50!*' Zara says in outrage. 'He only paid fifteen for it!'

Then she notices that Mr Reeve is standing in his doorway, and she moves nearer to Rob, wishing she'd spoken more quietly.

But Mr Reeve is indignant. 'How do you know how much I paid for it?' he demands.

'I was there, at the sale,' Zara says quietly. She does not add that she'd tried to bid for the bird and no one took any notice.

There are other people passing close by. They are within earshot, and Mr Reeve does not want his profits to be publicly discussed. 'Come inside,' he says.

Safely behind his counter – glass-topped and displaying around two hundred china animals – he faces his young accuser. 'I have to make a living,' he says plaintively.

'But that's more than three times as much as you paid!' The realities of profit-making are such a shock to Zara that she doesn't even think of handing over the conversation to Rob.

'What's more,' Mr Reeve says, 'I cleaned up a small part of it. *And* I mended the clockwork. Well, partly.'

'All the same,' Zara says, by no means mollified.

'Why? Are you interested in buying it?'

Then Zara tells him – resentfully – how she tried to bid for the bird but was unnoticed. Mr Reeve, however, pays little attention to her words. He is puzzled, lost in thought. Then, abruptly, he interrupts her.

'*I* know where I've seen your face!' he cries. 'You were on the telly! Both of you! Only a few days ago. You found that Roman ruin!'

He comes round to the front of his counter and shakes their hands vigorously. '*Maud!* Come in here a minute!'

Mrs Reeve is interested also and pleased to meet them. 'This lass wants to buy the musical box – you know, the bird in the cage.'

'A lovely object,' Mrs Reeve murmurs.

'You said it was *tat*! I heard you at the auction.'

Mrs Reeve smiles. 'That was when we were buying,' she says. 'Now we're selling.'

'I've got a £20 note,' Zara says. 'I will buy it for that.'

'Ridiculous!' Mrs Reeve says.

'But that would give you five pounds profit,' Zara points out.

'But I spent hours cleaning up the colours on that wing!' Mr Reeve says. 'Be fair!'

Rob thinks he can scrape together £5 to add to Zara's twenty. '£25,' he says.

'Final offer!' Zara adds.

Mr and Mrs Reeve are impressed by her command of the situation. (So is Rob.) And once the deal is done, they are all smiles and cheerfulness, allowing Zara and Rob to take away the bird now and bring the money next time they come to town. ('They only let us do that because we're famous,' Zara tells Rob later.)

'Have you really got that much money?' Mrs Reeve asks.

'I've got more than that,' Zara says proudly. 'In my bedroom. I've been saving up.'

Carefully, Zara nurses the bird as they manoeuvre their way across the crowded market square in search of Rob's mum. The boy in the hood sees what Zara is carrying. He smiles a narrow grin and says something incomprehensible. He has found a girlfriend, also wearing a black hood, also glowering ferociously. There are silver rings and studs in her lips and nostrils and eyebrows and a sparkly design of glossy green-and-black feathers curling over her cheeks and around her eyes. Her midriff is bare, and there's a silver ring in her navel. Zara is envious. *Does she have studs in her nipples and bells on her toes?* she wonders. She notices that they're holding hands as they lean against the wall of the library. Male and female hoodies. *Perhaps they will have a hoody baby*, she thinks.

*

That night Zara sits at the window in her bedroom. Outside, the night-time thrush has finished his trills and arpeggios and is settling down to more full-throated melodies. Inside, the metal bird is silent in its cage on Zara's windowsill.

'Use soap and warm water,' Mr Reeve had warned. 'Don't use a hard brush.' For hours and hours – all afternoon, in fact – Zara lovingly soaked away the dirt, realising with horrified disapproval that someone had painted the bird black.

'I will clean you completely,' she says to the bird. 'In time.'

She wonders if she could make it sing again too. When she wound it up – sitting on a seat in the churchyard waiting for Rob's mum to meet them – she found that Mr Reeve had, as he said, partly mended the clockwork. Now, she winds it again and releases the switch, and as the bird's tiny head moves delicately from side to side, its tail and wing feathers join in too, quivering up and down in silent excitement.

But its beak still opens and closes soundlessly.

It has been a long day. She switches her light off, does a gorilla leap onto her bed and pulls the covers around her shoulders.

There must be speaking, and there must be silence. The mechanical bird – for the time being – is part of the silence.

23

ALL TOGETHER NOW

Thomas awakes, listening in the night. There is a sharp, high squawking in the next room. Then another.

Father stirs and floorboards creak. Thomas listens. Mother murmurs, and the double squawking stops abruptly. He can see them in his mind's eye. Two tiny babies, two full breasts.

Two small walking sticks.

Out of bed and quickly across the splintery floor to the open window! Just in case he's there again! There is the smell of wallflowers, the chill of the night air, the black trees against the purple sky.

But there's no Banbury Giant tonight. No tall tale-teller in the road below Thomas's window. The lane is deep and still and silent.

Back to bed then! Quickly! So that he can think of

stories and books with stories stored in them. Of Tom Thumb, Robinson Crusoe, Jack the Giant-Killer and the children who lived in the forest with their best friends Robin Hood and Guy of Warwick.

We are in one place; we are in all places.
Sometimes we cheer you; sometimes we are churlish.
We hurt you, scare you and soothe you.

Sæwara, half-sleeping, wrapped close and tight in bed covers, riddles her words and stories. Making, remaking and memorising.

On the bedside table, the phone is sleeping. Downstairs in the kitchen, Mum's laptop sleeps too. But Zara is wide awake, her mind full of the last few days and their crowded busyness.

She thinks about a baby in a belly and the colour of a peacock's eye. She thinks about sitting on the sofa in her blue pyjamas and watching the ten o'clock news with Dad when she appeared (again!) and her voice rang out bright and true. Twice! Once on the national news and then again on the local.

A wonderful, lovely magic! Zara, speaking to her mum and dad out of the telly!

'You look very grown-up on television,' Dad said. 'I think you must have grown while I was away!'

Outside, the night is still and quiet. And a mystery has been solved: Mr Waller's thrush does *not* sing all through the night. He has fallen quiet at last, and the whole world is silent. For two hours after darkness fell, he broadcast his messages to the world. Now he is off-air, resting somewhere.

The mechanical bird is silent too. *Shall I?* Zara asks herself.

Molly Barnes, weary and safe in bed at last, is having a dream.

Only it's more like a vision than a dream. In a beautiful, low, stone-built house, she walks from room to room. In the dream, it belongs to her, but it's like no house she's ever been in. It's a low, long building, more like a small street than a house. Each room is spacious and filled with brilliant sunlight, connected to the next by steps that go up, or down, or round an unexpected corner.

It's full of people – some she knows; some are strangers. But she's happy to have them here, in her house.

'The trouble with Henry James,' she hears as she passes, 'is his sentences!' This makes her smile, happily.

There are lovely things in the rooms: vases filled with tall grasses and flowers, watercolours and prints on the walls, tapestries, collages, a beautiful carved wooden bowl containing small archaeological objects. 'Finger-pleasures,' she explains to one of the guests.

She's been searching for Abigail, and she finds her in Molly's favourite room, but she's cleared out all the furniture and is stripping off the wallpaper! *Why?* But Abigail just says, 'It needed doing!' and gets on with it.

Molly has no age in this dream. But she has clarity, definition. Completeness.

She steps outside into her courtyard, full of warm sunshine. Then back into the house by another door, into the kitchen, where she finds Adam has taken possession of the space, with an easel set up and a table with brushes and tubes and pots. He is painting a picture of three children on a radiant, sunny beach. Two of them are bending over a rock pool; the third – a little boy – is standing, watching them with his arms folded. People walk slowly around Adam, showing no interest in his painting, except a little girl, standing motionless, watching gravely. There's a three-legged cat sitting on a sunny windowsill, beside a crimson-flowered geranium in a flowerpot.

It's a bizarre, mad dream. But joyous, beyond all words!

Zara gets quietly out of bed, switches on her reading lamp and moves it onto the windowsill. Then she finds a nail file from her dressing table and turns the birdcage upside down on her lap. Using the file as a screwdriver, she removes four countersunk screws from the base and carefully takes off the circular metal cover.

As she works, she dislodges exhibit no.7 in her museum and three clay marbles roll, unnoticed, onto the carpet and under the radiator. Like three small animals scuttling quietly away, in search of a new home.

Zara is fascinated by the mechanisms that she finds assembled in the base under the bird: a tiny, neatly folded leather bellows and what seem to be wooden whistles with small rods and wheels. And when she winds it up, the wheels silently turn, and the rods move jerkily back and forth. They move the bird's head and beak, and the wings and tail, and pump the bellows in and out.

But all this mechanical energy produces no birdsong.

Not the faintest tweet! Just a feeble mechanical clatter, almost inaudible.

But Zara is confident. *I will make you sing again*, she promises. *I will work it out.*

She puts the bird through its motions three times, carefully studying the mechanism. Then she sees it! There is a small hole in the tiny bellows, where there is a fold in the soft leather. When she leans in close, she can feel tiny puffs of air, soft kisses blown through the hole and onto her cheek instead of into the whistles, where they belong.

She sets the clockwork going again, but this time she pinches the hole in the leather with her fingertips. This stops the air from leaking, and it goes instead where it's meant to go: into the wooden whistles. Immediately, the bird – not caring that it's upside down – bursts joyously into song, bubbling, trilling and pouring into the silence of Zara's bedroom… and out into the night because her window is open.

I can deal with that, she thinks. *I'll sew it up. Or glue it together. Or both, to make doubly sure.*

Sæwara, almost sinking into sleep, completes her story-teller's riddle.

> *We make things which are not there.*
> *We know when to begin and when to stop.*
> *We are in one place; we are in all places.*
> *Sometimes we cheer you; sometimes we are churlish.*
> *We hurt you, scare you and soothe you.*
> *We keep you awake; we send you to sleep.*
> *We make kings and queens, heroes and warriors –*

they are not there; they have no pith.
Brave men die in us who never lived.
Brave men live in us who died long ago.
We fill your minds with boys and girls,
men and women, kissing, killing, cooking –
they are phantoms, passing swiftly like birds.
We tell you falsehoods; we tell you truth.
We know when to begin and when to stop.
Now is the time to stop.

AUTHOR'S NOTE

Molly Barnes is one of the three central characters in Victor Watson's *Paradise Barn* novels for young readers. They are coming-of-age stories, set in World War Two. She is ten in the first of the series and sixteen in the last. That's when she realises she wants to be an archaeologist.

The five books are published by Catnip Press and can be ordered at bookshops and online.

Paradise Barn
The Deeping Secrets
Hidden Lies
Everyone a Stranger
Operation Blackout